A NATURAL TALENT

"Pull," cried Miss Bang.

Surprised, I reached for my gun as Tinka launched the skeet into the air. I watched the spinning clay disc as my hand snaked under my coat, and withdrew with the revolver held gently in my fingers. The gun felt light in my grasp. It fairly floated up in front of me as my eyes followed the pigeon. The pistol barked, and then dropped as fragments of clay scattered into the air. My hand snaked back up under my coat and stopped as the gun slid firmly back into its holster.

For several seconds, the only sound was that of the wind across the body of *the Argos*.

Tinka broke that silence. "Bloody hell!"

"Tinka, Language!"

She was unfazed at Miss Bang's rebuke. "Did you see that? Even with the bloody coat, the gun practically jumped into his hand. It was like he didn't have any bones! And he hit it." She turned to me. "You hit it like it was just sitting there."

"I know. It just... felt right." I shrugged.

"It would seem that the pistol is very much your weapon, my lord."

- from *Before Breakfast*

BOOKS BY DOC COLEMAN

The Adventures of Crackle and Bang

The Perils of Prague

The Kindred of Kali (coming soon)

Other Titles

The Shining Cog and Other Steampunk Tales

Other Short Stories

The Gift

Welcome to Paradox

DOC COLEMAN

THE SHINING COG

AND OTHER STEAMPUNK TALES

SWIMMING CAT STUDIOS

"The Cross of Columba" was first published by Imagine That! Studios in Tales from the Archives Volume 2, Episode 7 on October 30, 2012.
"The Blessing of the Cheese" was first published by A. F. Grappin in The Melting Potcast Episode 52 on November 1, 2017.
"A Walk in the Park" was first published by Flying Island Press as part of Flagship Magazine's Steampunk Special Issue on October 8, 2011.
"The Shining Cog" was first published by Iron Kilt Productions as part of the anthology *The Way of the Gun: A Bushido Western Anthology* on May 2, 2014
"Before Breakfast" and "Market Day" were first published in this volume on August 7, 2018.

Published in the United States of America by Swimming Cat Studios
https://SwimmingCatStudios.com

Cover design and cover art by Designed by Starla
(http://DesignedByStarla.com)
Some interior illustrations by Scott E. Pond Designs, LLC
(http://ScottPond.com)
Edited and proofed by Erin Kazmark

Print ISBN: 978-0-9980151-2-5
EBook ISBN: 978-0-9980151-3-2

PRINTED IN THE UNITED STATES OF AMERICA

10 9 8 7 6 5 4 3 2 1

FIRST EDITION: First printing - August 2018

DEDICATION

To Kee, my wife, for putting up with me for over 25 years.
For dealing with my madness as I sought to find my voice and my art.
For letting me build these crazy worlds instead of helping cleaning up the house.
For bringing me back to ground when I'm stressed.
For pitching in to help when I've taken on too much. Again.
For being my sounding board when the ideas don't flow.
For being my first reader and my last reader.
For giving me your opinions, even if I don't agree.
I dedicate this book to you.
I love you.

ACKNOWLEDGMENTS

This book wouldn't be possible without the help of a number of people who donated their particular skills and insights to make the pieces all come together. So I'd like to take this moment to express my thanks to the following people:

Pip Ballantine and Tee Morris - For letting me play in your world and bring a new dimension to the Ministry. I love the world you've created and would like to play there again. But next time, edit harder.

August Grappin - For being a sneak and bringing in special voice talent for "The Blessing of the Cheese". You rock.

Starla Huchton - For creating some beautiful cover art very quickly, and putting up with all my less than educated suggestions. Thank you.

Julayne Hughes - For the original edits for "The Shining Cog". It helped improve the story a lot.

Erin Kazmark - For being a good friend, and a speedy editor. I expect I'll be one of the first of many clients for your new endeavor.

Scott Pond - For your amazing art that perfectly offsets a Crackle and Bang story.

Zachary Ricks and the staff of Flying Island Press - For encouraging me to write, and for accepting my first Steampunk short story. See what you started!

Scott Roche - For inviting me to play in your world, and letting me run with it and make something special.

CONTENTS

A WALK IN THE PARK

THE SHINING COG

AN EXCERPT FROM THE PERILS OF PRAGUE

FOREMOST (THE ONLY ONE YOU HAVE TO READ.)

Thank you, dear reader, for picking up this book.

If you're a lover of steampunk, of adventure, or if you've read some of my other stories and wanted to see more, or even if you just picked this book up because it looked interesting, I think you're in for a treat. Of course, I might be a tad biased.

At the beginning and end of each story, you'll find a Foreword / Afterword. These provide a little extra information about the stories, and how they came about. If you're really just interested in the stories themselves, you can just skip these. Think of them as bonus material.

But enough of that. Six stories await.

Enjoy the Adventure!

THE CROSS OF COLUMBA

FOREWORD

This first story was written for Tee Morris and Pip Ballentine's *Tales from the Archives* podcast. It is part of a collection of short stories written in their excellent steampunk world where the British Crown sponsors a secret Ministry to investigate strange and unusual events and protect the Empire from their causes.

Each story is a case file from the archives of the Ministry, detailing an investigation recorded by one of their agents. The investigation could occur anywhere in the Empire, or any other part of the world where you would be likely to find a British Agent.

I chose Scotland... and that meant I needed to come up with something special.

THE CROSS OF COLUMBA

April 9th, 1883

The mist that rose off the lake cut the small boat off from the rest of the world. With the moon obscured by clouds, and the sun having set behind the rolling highlands, a single lantern mounted on a pole at the bows provided the only illumination in their tiny world. Lord Ansley Curtis Belgrave Pennyfarthing stood in the bow of the tiny rowboat, his rifle in his hands. His eyes were fixed on the wall of mist trying pierce the veil and gain some glimpse of his quarry.

"M'lord," the voice of the boy in the stern of the boat carried clearly over the still waters, although he spoke in little more than a whisper. "It's late, m'lord. Shouldna we head back to shore? We canna see nuthin' in this fog." The fourteen-year-old boy shivered in the cooling night air, the chill finally catching up with his apprehension.

"Hush!" the noble replied, ignoring the fact that his booming voice was much louder than the boy's plaintive question. "Listen, Robbie," Lord Pennyfarthing said lifting his rifle to his shoulder, but not taking aim. "The beast is out there. I can hear it!"

Robbie listened, but could hear nothing other than the water dripping off of his oars and the chattering of his teeth. The boy tucked his hands up under his armpits and tried to warm them with the remaining heat in his body.

The boat swayed slightly, causing the lantern to swing, and raising Robbie from his drowsy state. The fog bank remained unchanged and no wind stirred, but gentle waves began to lap against the boat. Lord Pennyfarthing adjusted his stance, threatening a different stretch of innocent fog with his weapon. The waves continued to lap against the boat, slapping it with greater energy, and making the lantern dance on the end of its pole. Robbie pulled the oars inside the boat and held onto his seat as the boat rocked beneath him. The lord continued to menace the mist with his weapon, muttering, "Come on, old girl. Show yourself."

Robbie could still hear the drip-drip of water, but with the oars inside the boat, where could it be coming from? The boy looked up at the dome of fog, and started to find a dark, scaly head staring back at him. Water dripped from the open jaws of the creature as it regarded the boy in the boat with small shining eyes. The head was easily as large as the boat, and the creature could have snapped up Robbie in a single bite.

The boy backed away from the creature and let out a strangled squeak. Lord Pennyfarthing snapped his attention from the thick fog in front of him to the giant head above him. He raised his rifle and squeezed off a shot that rang out in the darkness. Despite the rifle's power and the close range, the bullet bounced off the thick hide of the creature, leaving it otherwise unharmed. The sudden noise, however, startled the leviathan; it reared and let out a roar that echoed back from the hills on either side of the lake.

The boy turned and leapt from the boat into the cold water of the lake, swimming for the unseen shoreline in his panic to be away from the creature. With Robbie's departure, the boat rocked wildly under Lord Pennyfarthing, topping him over onto his back in the small vessel. The lord didn't bother to try to right himself, but fired again, twice in quick succession from his position sprawled upon his back.

Another roar punctuated the night, and the creature struck out at the small boat. The lantern flared briefly and then was extinguished as it fell into the water. Robbie heard a single scream from the English lord, which was cut off suddenly amid the sounds of the wooden boat being shattered under the creature's attack. The boy redoubled his efforts, swimming madly into the darkness.

April 10th, 1883
Special Agent Bryan Sebastian Teague was not happy. And he was wet. Very, very wet.

When Teague had first been approached by the Ministry for a position, he had been told that they needed his zoological expertise to identify and preserve rare and unusual species in their native habitats. He was promised the chance to travel the world and be part of some of the most premiere zoological research on the planet. When he accepted the position with the Ministry of the Strange and Unusual, he found himself assigned as the one-man department of cryptozoology. Instead of being part of serious research, he was stuck at a desk, reading outrageously fantastic reports from other agents who had allegedly encountered new species in the field.

The worst of these reports were the ones that contained "specimens". More often than not these were chunks of mangled meat that hadn't been properly preserved. Even the specimens that were well preserved had been so damaged by gunfire, explosives, and other mayhem that they were unrecognizable as little more than meat.

And then Lord Pennyfarthing came along.

Ansley Curtis Belgrave Pennyfarthing was one of those petty lordlings that considered himself to be a scientist and an explorer because he could afford to hire a guide and carry a big gun. What brought Lord Pennyfarthing to the Ministry's attention was the type of game that he hunted for. Agent Teague's first field assignment had him traveling to Greece to verify Lord Pennyfarthing's claim to have captured an actual Chimera. What he found on display at Lord Pennyfarthing's press conference had convinced him that his lordship would be well served to find a more skilled taxidermist and fresher samples when attempting to pull off a hoax. The creature in question appeared to have been a museum piece of a lion that had been retired from display due to extreme old age and mange, to which the head of a goat and the body of a snake had been tacked on with little regard to aesthetics or anatomy.

Lord Pennyfarthing was not deterred after having his "find" debunked. Indeed he appeared to re-double his efforts to discover some mythical creature or another. For the past year, Agent Teague's life had been spent chasing after Lord Pennyfarthing and exposing his latest discovery as yet another fraud. This might have been interesting work for some, but Teague yearned for the chance to do some real research.

Preferably research that did not involve a trip to Scotland.

The train from London to Inverness had been the most enjoyable part of this latest excursion. The problems began when he arrived at Inverness Station and discovered that the carriage that he had hired to take him to Drumnadrochit Village turned out to be an open farm cart returning to the village after delivering a load of manure, or something else equally foul smelling. Teague had been unable to either get his money refunded, or to hire any alternative transportation.

The farmer driving the cart hadn't even noticed when the rains began shortly after they left Inverness for the twelve mile trip to the village. Now, after over two hours of riding in the rain, Agent Teague was soaked to the bone. His hat drooped like a sodden rag, the brim falling into his face and channeling the rain onto his shoulders. As the cart finally arrived in the village, Teague was hard put to decide which he hated more, Scotland, or Lord Pennyfarthing.

The cart pulled up in front of the lone inn in the village, and the farmer grunted, apparently feeling that was sufficient to announce that they had arrived. Teague lifted his bags from his lap and feet, having decided he would rather clutch them through the nearly three hour long ride rather than trust them to the dubious state of the back of the open wagon. Teague stepped down from the front of the wagon to the cobblestoned road of the village. As the cold water from the street ran into his shoes, he mentally adjusted the balance of his hatred in Lord Pennyfarthing's favour.

Teague entered the inn, looking, he was sure, much like a drowned rat. He stopped just inside the closed door, water continuing to pour off him into a spreading pool on the inn's stone floor. "Heavens, lovey, whot did ye' do, fall into the loch?" a matron called from behind the bar of the inn's large common room.

Rough laughter echoed from the handful of men scattered about the room. The structure appeared to double as the local public house with food and drink served downstairs and rooms available for rent on the upper floors. The matron pushed open a door at the end of the bar and called into the room beyond, "Colin! Grab a mop and come clean this up." She smiled as she turned back to Teague. "Don't worry, 'bout the mess, lovey, just set ye'self down by the fire for a bit 'an dry off."

"Thank, you ma'am," the agent answered, "but if you have a room available, I think I'd like to change into some dry clothes."

"Oh, certainly, lovey!" she replied with genuine hospitality. A middle-aged man emerged from the back room, a mop in hand. The matron called to him, "Colin, show this gent up to number four. Just leave that mop here." She turned back to Teague, "Go get ye'self cleaned up, lovey, we'll get you all checked in proper when you're done."

Colin propped his mop up in a corner and came over to take Teague's bags from him, frowning briefly at the damp handles. "This way, sir." He said, then turned and stomped up the flight of stairs in the far corner of the room. Teague winced at the squishing noise his shoes made as he walked across the stone floor of the common room and up the squeaky wood stairs in Colin's wake.

Agent Teague continued to wish for a change of dry clothes, but resigned himself to settling for clothing that was merely damp. The rain had soaked through his cases and touched every bit of his wardrobe. His room was now adorned with hanging clothing on each surface in an attempt to draw the moisture out. He was feeling some-what better after a warm shower, and the chance to deplete some of the Inn's supply of dry towels.

His shoes still squelched with each step, his weight pushing more moisture out of the soaked leather, as Teague went back downstairs to the common room of the inn. He signed the guest ledger under the cheerful eye of the landlady, refusing her offer of a meal to help warm him, but gratefully accepting a hot cup of tea.

"What brings ye to our little village, lovey? We don't get too many visitors in these parts." The other patrons of the inn seemed glad of this fact, but it was apparent that the landlady, for one, was happy to have someone new to talk to.

"Word has reached London that Lord Pennyfarthing has made some sort of major zoological discovery in the lake here. I've been dispatched from the government to verify the veracity of Lord Penny-farthing's find. Do you know where I might be able to find his lord-ship?" Agent Teague hoped this business could be finished quickly and he could put this god-forsaken patch of Scotland behind him and return to London, and civilization.

The landlady's expression showed her opinion of Lord Pennyfar-thing, one which Teague could readily agree with. "Och, You're looking for his nibs? He's probably still out chasing snarks and boojums on the loch. Last I heard he and Robbie Spencer were taking a boat out on the loch to search for that beastie of his. They're not going to find nothing but mist on that loch at night, mark my words, lovey." She stopped for a moment and looked thoughtful. "Although, Robbie usually comes by each morning to take his lordship's breakfast up to him, and I dinna seem him his morning…"

One of the other patrons spoke up from his seat near the fire. "Dinna ye hear, Maggie? Robbie's up at the docs. Seems their boat sank last night. Poor lad had te swim his way to shore. They found the poor bairn washed up on the beach this morning, chilled right through. His mam took him right up to the docs and they laid him te bed."

"Oh, the poor dear!" the landlady cried.

Teague turned to the man, "Was there any word of his lordship?"

The man shook his head and turned back to his pint. "Nay. We figgur his nibs must have drowned in the loch."

"Where is your physician's office?" Teague asked of the landlady.

"It's just up the high street, lovey. Oh, I hope the poor boy will be all right."

Teague turned and headed back out into the Scottish rain,

wondering if this time Pennyfarthing had actually found something real, or if his folly had finally caught up with him.

The visit to the doctor's yielded rather disappointing results; he'd refused to allow Teague to talk to the boy, stating that the child was with fever and wasn't able to speak coherently in any case. The man was a stubborn Scot and wasn't even swayed by government credentials. Teague had learned something of use from the nurse, however. The Spencer boy had indeed been hired by Lord Pennyfarthing when his lordship came to town. While his lordship was lodged at the inn, the two of them spent most of their time at a camp Pennyfarthing had set up. Some tents on a hill overlooking the lake by the old ruined castle.

Thankfully, the rain stopped while Agent Teague made his way down to the shoreline. Feeling almost dry, the agent inspected the small encampment. Two tents had been pitched, side-by-side on a hummock overlooking the lake. One tent contained a cot and a few personal belongings; the other had been set up with one side open to the lake, providing an excellent view of the water for miles. Just down the shoreline stood a tower and a partial wall of an ancient fortification, the rest of the structure having been turned into scattered stones over the years. Teague had no doubt that the site for the castle had likewise been chosen for the excellent view.

In the back of this tent were a number of crates. Some had been opened and appeared to contain supplies for the camp. The fire pit had been drowned in the rain, but still had a tripod over it, and a camp pot perched over where the fire should have been. In another long crate, Teague found a heavy caliber rifle and several boxes of ammunition. There was also a void in the packing materials of the crate where another rifle should have been.

Teague righted one of the camp chairs, brushed off the dirt, and sat himself down upon it. "What did you think you had found, Pennyfarthing?" Teague mumbled to himself.

"Halloooo!" came a call from behind the tent.

Teague exited and found an old man making his way down the path from the road to the camp. He was a grizzled looking Scot with wisps of grey hair sticking out from under a battered oilskin hat on his head. He was wearing a stained and weathered Mackintosh over his dark clothing, and sturdy boots, caked with mud. As the he drew near, Teague spotted the white clerical collar peeping through the open collar of his raincoat.

"Ah," the old priest said. "I thought ye were his lordship. I'm Father Graham Blackmore, from the chapel," he gestured up the hill at a weathered stone building that could barely be seen through the trees. "I was on my way into town to take tea at Maggie's. Thought I'd invite his lordship to give up his fairy chasing, and join me for a cup. Are you an associate of his lordship's?"

Teague extended his hand and was rewarded with a strong handshake from the priest. "I'm Agent Bryan Teague from the government. I've been sent here to verify Lord Pennyfarthing's find, but it seems that now his lordship himself has gone missing. Did you speak with him often, Father?"

"Oh, aye. I come by here just about every day. We'd have a good chat, and I'd try to get him to give up this fools errand, but his lordship is a stubborn man, an' sure there is somethin' more than fish to be found in the loch. Now he's missing, you say?"

Teague ignored the question, and pressed on with one of his own. "Do you know what Lord Pennyfarthing was looking for, Father?"

The elderly priest went and sat on one of the campstools. "Pish and nonsense, my boy. This area has been full of folklore and superstition. Fishermen seeing shapes in the mist and telling tall tales in the pub. His lordship was sure that there was somethin' behind all the tales." He turned to look back up at the agent. "I tried to tell him that all the lochs in this area have similar tales and that there was nothin' to 'em but a good yarn around the cook fires, but he wouldn'a listen to an old priest like me. Do we know wha' happened to him?"

"Apparently, Lord Pennyfarthing and the Spencer boy went out on the lake in a small boat last night, and it sank. The boy made it back to shore, but he's feverish. The doctor says he isn't giving a coherent account of what happened. No sign of his lordship or the boat."

"Oh, dear. Thank you for letting me know. I'd better get into town and see what I can do for Robbie and his mam. Why don't you come with me, Mr. Teague? I might be able to find out what happened from Robbie. No use sitting out here in the wind if you don't have to."

The agent considered the priest's offer, but decided that there might still be clues here in the camp. "Thank you, Father, but I believe I still have work here. Although I would appreciate it if you could convince the doctor to let me speak with the Spencer boy."

The priest grunted as he stood. "Very well. If you've set your mind, I'll see what I can do without you. Could you at least give me a hand back up to the road?"

The agent agreed and, taking the priest's arm, the two of them made their way up the muddy path to the road that ran parallel to the shore of the lake. As the pair achieved their goal, a horse drawn cart came down the road, moving quickly. Upon seeing the two of them at the roadside, the driver pulled back on the reins, bringing the cart up along side them. The horse huffed and snorted as the driver called down to them. "Father Graham! They pulled his lordship from the loch! The man's been hurt awful bad, Father. Tha doc says he's nae gonna make it."

Teague helped the priest up into the cart, and then scrambled up next to him. "I've decided to take you up on your offer, Father." The driver carefully turned the cart about in the middle of the lane, and then they set back off to the village at a trot.

Following along in Father Graham's wake, Teague made his way into the small hospital and was led to the room where Lord Pennyfarthing had been brought. The doctor looked at the priest mournfully. "There is nothin' I can do father. His leg has been taken off and the infection has run all through him. It is a miracle he's lasted this long. I've given him morphine for the pain, but he's not stable enough for me to do much else."

The priest put a hand on the doctor's shoulder. "I understand, my son. You did what you could, now let us see what we can do to ease his passing." The doctor gave Teague a sharp look, but didn't argue when the two men stepped into the room.

The room was filled with the smell of lake water, and the stench of infection. Lord Pennyfarthing lay on a hospital bed, still wet from the lake. His right leg ended abruptly right above where his knee should have been. A leather belt had been tied around the truncated thigh and drawn tight, squeezing the colour from the pallid flesh of his leg. The fabric of his pants had been cut away from the belt, and sickly green stains could be seen beneath the skin.

Teague, covering his mouth and nose with a handkerchief, moved to the bedside and began to examine the wound. The tear was ragged and appeared to the agent's eye to have been caused by something with large, curved teeth. The priest stepped up to the left side of the bed and laid a gentle hand on the fevered man's shoulder. Lord Penny-farthing's eyes flashed open and his hand shot out and grabbed the priest by the collar. Pulling the old man close, the lord spoke with a frantic intensity, "I found it, Father! I found it! It's real!"

Moving up to Pennyfarthing's head, the agent tried to disengage the lord's grip on the priest. Father Graham made a placating gesture to Teague, but addressed his words to Pennyfarthing, "What did you find, Ansley?"

The wounded man turned to the agent and grabbed his shoulder with his right hand. "Teague! You won't make a laughing stock of me this time, boy! I found it, it's real!"

Teague looked into his eyes, seeing a mania that had consumed the man's entire being. "What did you find?" he asked, feeling some of that mania seeping into himself.

"A beast! A mighty beast in the loch! A great serpent that hides beneath the water. I've seen it! Its head is as big as a man, and it bit through my leg and the boat as if they weren't there. Bullets just bounced off of its hide! You must hunt it! Bring it to ground! You owe me that much, Teague. Show the world what I've found! Pennyfar-thing's Monster! Show them the truth. The legends are true. These creatures are everywhere!" The man gasped, digging his fingers into Teague's shoulder. He pulled himself up briefly from the bed, and then collapsed back onto its surface in a limp heap. The agent put his fingers to the side of the lord's neck, drawing upon the basic medical training the Ministry required for all agents. Unable to find a pulse, Teague folded the man's hands over his chest. Turning to the priest, he said, "I believe he is now in your care, Father."

The priest reached under his vest and pulled out a large gold cross, engraved with knot work and worn smooth around the edges with the handling of many hands. As the priest began to pray, Teague turned and walked from the room. He called for the doctor; informing the man that his lordship appeared to have passed.

April 11th, 1883
The fire crackled in a freshly dug fire pit, stocked with firewood that had been stashed inside one of the empty crates. Agent Teague checked the rifle again, trying to assure himself that it was indeed clean and ready to fire. He had never been comfortable with firearms, but it seemed better than his other alternative. His eyes slid to a small crate that sat at the edge of the firelight, and the three sticks of dynamite that sat upon it for easy access. He didn't dare move the explosives any closer to the fire, and he was afraid that he'd end up blowing himself to pieces as it was.

Teague directed his eyes back out over the lake. Night had closed in quickly in the highlands, and for once, the clouds had cleared. Moonlight reflected off the water of the lake, making it shimmer in the cold night air. He swept his gaze over the water, searching for some sign of the beast.

His instructions from the Director had been clear. Debunk the find if possible, but if Pennyfarthing's discovery turned out to be real, secure a sample for the Ministry; live if possible, but dead if necessary. Should the creature prove to be dangerous, death will be required. Teague thought of himself as a scientist. He was not comfortable with the role of a hunter, but there was no denying that this creature had proven to be dangerous.

The snap of bracken behind him sent Teague spinning around, the rifle raised to his shoulder and ready to fire. He halted as he saw that the cause was the old priest. Father Graham raised his hands. "It's just me, son. No reason to fire."

Teague lowered the weapon and turned back to face the water. "What are you doing out here, Father? It's not safe."

"I can see that," the priest replied. "Why don't you come with me? My place is not far. We can discuss this over a nice glass of whiskey."

"I have work to do here, Father. The government sent me to collect a sample if this find proved to be real. That is what I am here to do." Teague paced down the hill, his steps crunching on the stones of the shoreline, the water of the lake lapping a few feet from him.

The old man moved down to stand next to Teague, looking at him with piercing eyes. "You don't want to do this, my son. You're not that kind of man. You admire God's creatures, you're not one to kill them. Give it up, son. If there is something in the loch, maybe it is better off left where it is. Leave it be, son."

"You saw what that thing did to Lord Pennyfarthing, Father. The man was an ass, but he didn't deserve that. While this thing lives, everyone in this town is in danger, possibly everyone along the shores of the lake. It is a clear danger to the Empire. I have to take care of it."

"What if there is something worse, lad? A greater danger. Something that this creature keeps in check? If you kill this creature, you could be unleashing a worse terror on the world!" The priest's voice rang out over the lake like a sermon in nature's own cathedral.

"You sound as if you know about this, Father. You've been discouraging my investigation every step of the way. Is this monster some doing of yours? Are you the cause of it? Is that man's death on your hands?"

"No!" the old priest cried. "It's not like that, lad. No one was ever meant to be hurt! You don't understand, boy. Some secrets are meant to be secret!"

"I deal in secrets, Father. What are you hiding?"

"Boy, ye're meddlin' in things that ye just don' understa—" The priest cut off in mid harangue, and clutched at his chest before tumbling to the ground like a felled tree.

Teague rushed over to the old man, going down on one knee, and placing the rifle on the ground. "You'd better not be faking, Father."

The priest was breathing heavily. He fumbled around his neck, pulling out the heavy cross that Teague had seen at the hospital. "Bad heart. I... I don't have much time," he gasped. "It has to be you." Slipping the chain over his head, he pushed the cross into Teague's hand. "The truth, now, boy. I am the last of the Order of Columba. We have protected the secret of the loch for centuries. Now, it has to be you. A beast has been imprisoned beneath the lake, but with my death, it will try to escape." He struggled to catch his breath, and then closed Teague's fingers around the cross. "Take the cross. With it you can call upon the guardian. Use it to keep the beast at bay. The beast will come for me." His fingers tightened on Teague's hand and he levered himself up to stare into Teague's eyes. "It must not get the cross!" The old man slumped back. Teague caught him with one hand and tucked the cross into his pocket. "It all depends on you..." His voice fading out with his final breath, the old priest died in Teague's arms.

Teague checked his neck for a pulse, but could find no sign of life. He closed the priest's eyes, and placed his hands over his chest. "Rest in peace, Father."

Teague stood and retrieved the cross from his pocket. It was about five inches long, and three wide, and decorated with intricate knot work. Small gems were set into each of the cardinal points, but what appeared to be a common stone was set in the center of the cross. Teague was about to place it back on the priest's chest, when a mournful cry echoed off the hills and over the lake. Something in the darkness was expressing its grief, a keening cry raised to the sky. Teague stuffed the cross into his pocket and grabbed his rifle back up again. Backing his way up the small hill, the agent pointed his gun out over the water. He remembered the priest's warning that the beast would come for him.

The water of the lake began to bubble and boil, the shoreline directly in front of the agent frothing as some gigantic monstrosity thrust itself up to the surface. Flopping through the dark waters, the thing drew into sight, heaving itself from the water onto the shore. Teague's mind reeled as he tried to take in the abomination. The creature appeared to be assembled from the pieces of hundreds of bodies, melded together into an unholy imitation of life. Rotted cloth hung from it in some places, while in others, ancient armor still clung to bodies that should have dissolved centuries ago. Helmets of Roman legionnaires remained strapped to the lolling heads of soldiers over a thousand years gone. The monster stretched out across the shoreline, thrusting itself forward on hands, feet, and other appendages that defied description. Its body extended for yards back into the frothing water. The stench of death and corruption made Teague gag and retch.

The agent raised the rifle and fired three shots into the mass of the abomination. The bullets ripped into it, but as soon as the holes formed, the flesh of the beast sealed them back over. Undeterred, it flopped its way further onto the bank.

The agent turned and ran up the bank to the circle of firelight. He dropped the rifle to the ground and grabbed up the three sticks of dynamite. He lit the fuse of the first stick, then flung it at the creature, then repeated the action a second and third time. The dynamite arced down onto the body of the creature, then detonated with three booming explosions. The blasts ripped gaping holes in the mass, and rained down severed limbs over the monster.

Teague gaped in astonishment as the severed limbs grafted themselves back into the mass where they fell, often while pointed in the wrong direction. Pieces that fell apart from the monstrosity bound to each other, and flopped around on the shore, reaching back towards the central mass. As he stared in disbelief the wounds refilled themselves, strange worm-like masses pulling parts of bodies from the other sections of the beast.

The thing continued to flop forward onto the shore, but came to a stop when it approached the body of Father Graham. As Agent Teague looked on in revulsion, the abomination reached out with dead arms and grabbed the corpse, lifting it up against its own mass. Wormlike appendages pushed from the body of the horror and hooked into the priest's flesh. As they burrowed into the dead man, his body jerked and shuddered. Eventually, he was grafted into the mass of the monster on the beach. The old priest's limbs began moving again, and his eyes opened and rolled. A low groan emitted from the priest's mouth.

Teague stumbled backwards, tripping in his haste and sprawling onto the ground. The beast resumed its progress, flopping its monstrous body further onto the shoreline, random arms and legs seeking purchase to drag its bulk from the water.

Scrambling backwards, the agent remembered the cross in his pocket. He dug it out, and brandished it at the abomination. Trying desperately to remember the words of the priest, Teague held the cross high, and called out, "Guardian! Guardian, I need your help!" not knowing what he expected to happen.

A stentorian roar echoed across the lake. The metal of the cross burnt Teague's hand, searing into his flesh. He tried to release it, but strangely his hand only gripped the metal tighter. Visions of rushing water filled Teague's mind and a blinding light like a beacon flared ahead of him. Through the tears in his eyes, Teague saw the beast hesitate for a moment, then throw itself forward with greater urgency, franticly trying to gain the shore.

A great reptilian head burst forth from the water at the end of a long, muscular neck and arced down into the midst of the beast, biting into the tainted flesh of the horror. A foul taste filled Teague's mouth, making him want to gag and spit. He swore that something was fighting against his tongue. The reptile twisted its neck, lifting up the monstrosity and tossing it back into the lake. The agent's eyes rolled back into his head. He fell to the ground, overwhelmed as his mind was filled with the emotions and senses of the reptilian creature. In his mind he saw the creature take its anger—their anger—out on the abomination, beating the unholy thing back from the shore, hammering it with heavy blows from head and tail and flipper. With their powerful, scaled body, they drove it into the lake, folding it back onto itself until it collapsed into an uncoordinated ball.

Grabbing the foul-tasting creature in their mouth, they dove, pushing it into the depths of the lake. Down, down, into the darkness, driving it into the murky depths. In the very deepest part of the lake, they pounded the monster into the mud at the bottom, miring it. Then with a powerful thrust, they rose up along the submerged cliffs, hammering against the stones. Under this repeated attack the cliff shattered, raining boulders down to bury the beast.

Their fury and grief spent, they swam for the surface again, rising through the waters in mighty strokes. Their head breached the surface, and together they breathed in the sweet pre-dawn air over the loch. The danger over for the moment, they relaxed, and returned to their separate selves.

Teague came to himself lying on his back on the shore. The light morning rain fell on him as dawn tinged the horizon. As he blinked the rain out of his eyes, Teague levered himself onto his elbows and laughed at the overcast skies. The cross was still clutched in his hand.

The agent sat up and slipped the cross' chain over his neck. He looked at his hand. He could still feel the echo of the burn, but the flesh seemed whole and intact. His hand only seemed a little stiff from clutching the cross all night.

Teague climbed back to his feet and looked out over the waters of the loch for a moment. Then he turned and began walking back to the village.

May 17th, 1883
The door to the study creaked loudly as it opened, but the man behind the desk continued writing without even looking up. "Robbie, I told you to knock before coming into my study."

"I'll be sure to remind him if I should see him,"

Agent Teague looked up in surprise at the rotund man standing just inside the door to the study. His appearance gave the impression of joviality, although that impression didn't extend to his eyes, which seemed to pierce Teague to the very core. The Agent stood and addressed his visitor. "Doctor Sound. What a surprise. I wasn't aware that you still went out into the field, sir."

"Normally, I don't have to. But then again, normally my agents don't refuse to return from the field at the conclusion of an investigation."

Teague shifted uncomfortably. "Ah, I'm afraid, Director, that I now have responsibilities here that require my presence. Responsibilities that cannot be set aside, sir."

Doctor Sound stepped further into the room, and approached the antique wood desk located in the center of the small space. He seated himself in one of the two chairs facing the desk and took a moment to glance at the stuffed bookshelves that covered the walls of the small study. He leaned back in the chair, considering Teague for a moment before answering. "Would these new responsibilities have something to do with the fact that when I asked after you in the village, they sent me here to find 'Father Bryan'?"

Teague coloured momentarily. "I'm afraid that is the doing of my predecessor, Father Graham." He picked up a leather-bound book from the desk and handed it to the Director. "He was the last member of a secret order that called itself the Brotherhood of Columba. He spent some time telling the villagers that in the event of his death, the call would come to one of them and they would have to take over his parish." Teague sat. "When they saw me come in with Father Graham's cross, they decided that the call had come to me and I was now Father Bryan." He rubbed his forehead. "I guess in a way, I did receive a calling."

Sound looked at the younger man. "And this new spiritual calling is what is keeping you here?"

"Not exactly, sir. Did you read the report that I sent in?"

Sound steepled his fingers. "Yes, but I wanted to hear it from you myself."

"Lord Pennyfarthing had indeed found a creature in the loch. What he did not know is that the creature was here for a purpose. Something else is imprisoned in the loch. Something that the Brotherhood referred to as 'the demon'. The creature is here as a guardian, to keep the demon from escaping, and the Brotherhood was created to protect the creature."

"To protect it?"

"Yes, sir. From the prying eyes of men. From those who would hunt it. Or use it."

"And now this Brotherhood of Columba is gone," Sound replied.

"Except for me, Director."

"You believe that this supersedes your duty to the Ministry, then, Teague?"

The agent bowed his head, then looked up at the Director of the

Ministry of the Strange and Unusual. "Doctor Sound, you sent me out here to secure a sample for the Ministry if Lord Pennyfarthing's find proved to be real. I have done so. The creature is real, and I have secured it on behalf of the Ministry. It also turns out that it is vitally important to the safety of the Empire, possibly the world, for the creature to remain here. And since I took up the Cross of Columba, I have been bonded to the creature, and I must remain here as well. Watching over it, and keeping it hidden from the world." He gestured to the books surrounding them on the walls. "These are the accounts of my predecessors, going back centuries. I have barely begun to scratch the lore here, sir, but everything I have found so far makes two things clear. I will have to watch over the loch for the rest of my life, and when I die, someone will have to take up the cross. Otherwise we will unleash something unspeakable on the Empire."

"Bonded, you said? In what way?"

The agent smiled. "I can feel the creature in the back of my head. If I concentrate, I can sense what she senses. It is a little like being in two places at once. I can guide her, keep her away from prying eyes."

"Her?"

"Yes, the creature is a female, sir"

"And the attack on Lord Pennyfarthing?"

"From what I've been able to gather, he was actively hunting her at night. My best guess is that Father Graham was asleep when the attack happened and was unable to properly control her." Teague removed a heavy cross on a chain around his neck and placed it on the desk between them.

"This is the artifact?"

"Yes, Director. The Cross of Columba."

Doctor Sound leaned in to look at the gilded cross. He reached one pudgy hand towards it, but checked himself before touching it. He looked at Teague under heavy brows. "Is it safe?"

"Yes, sir. For you, it is quite safe, as long as I am alive." Sound hesitated a moment longer, then picked up the cross. Teague continued, "From what I've read in the more recent records, the cross appears to have just one function. It forms a bond between the guardian and the person that holds the cross. Once the bond is formed, it lasts until death. So when I die, someone had better be around to take up the cross."

Sound flipped the cross over and examined the engravings on the back. "That's all? It just forms the bond and nothing else?"

The agent sighed. "That is all we know for sure. I've come across some speculation from past holders that the cross somehow uses the bond to keep the demon confined to the lake. The demon is aware of the cross. When the old holder dies, it comes straight for the cross. If it gets to the cross first, there may be no caging it again. It may even be able to control the guardian." He shook his head. "I'd rather not think about that."

"Then I should take this back to London for safe keeping." Sound started to fit the cross into his pocket.

"NO!" Teague jumped forward, then stopped himself. "I can't leave the loch, but I can't leave the cross either. I left it by my bedside one morning and I barely got out the door. I am bound to it as much as I am to the lake." He held his hand out for the cross. After a moment, Sound solemnly returned it.

"You're not giving me a lot of options here, Agent Teague. That is a position I do not like to be put in by my agents."

"I'm sorry, sir."

Sound considered the man for a long moment as Teague returned the cross to its place around his neck. The Director then grunted and pushed himself back to his feet. "It would seem that I have little choice. You are correct in one matter, Teague. You have acquired a valuable asset for the Ministry—one which we need to protect. This is what we are going to do. Effective immediately, you are now assigned to the Scottish branch of the Ministry, on permanent detached duty to Loch Ness. You'll coordinate through the Inverness office. I'll have their archivist contact you about securing translations of these histories." He considered a moment longer, then asked, "How do you intend to deal with the church?"

"This parish has a long history of lay ministers, sir. It is small enough not to gather too much notice, and there seems to be an understanding of sorts with the bishop."

"Just don't expect me to bail you out of trouble with the church, 'vicar'." Sound turned and walked to the door of the small study.

"Director!" The portly man stopped with his hand on the doorknob and turned back to Teague. "Thank you for your understanding, sir. I... well, I don't plan on dying any time soon, but when it does happen..." he trailed off.

"Yes. I'll arrange for an assistant to watch over you. Perhaps this might make a good first field experience for young agents, hmmmm?" One corner of Sound's mouth twitched upwards at the idea.

"Thank you, sir."

"Just make sure that once they leave here they don't give me as much trouble as you have. I promise you I will not be so lenient in the future." The Director jerked the study door open with a squeal. He started to leave, but then turned back for one final remark. "And for God's sake, name these things! If you're going to report on a monster in Loch Ness, I want to know which one you're talking about. No more of this 'beast' and 'creature' nonsense. Give them proper names."

With that, Sound exited the study, letting the door slam behind him. The agent turned priest sat down at his desk and considered this last request from the director. "Names for the Loch Ness monsters, eh?" He smiled. "Ness. Nessie?" Father Bryan liked the sound of that. Old Nessie. He was pretty sure that she'd like it, too. He'd have to look up some appropriately biblical name for the demon of the loch, but that could wait until later. He reached out to her with his mind, calling out to Nessie. She answered with images of cool waters, and a feeling of pleasure. She accepted the name. Together they were Nessie.

AFTERWORD

When Tee and Pip offered me the opportunity to write in their world, I was ecstatic. Tee had been telling me about the series that *Tales from the Archives* is based off of since they started working on the very first book, and it intrigued me greatly. I could not wait to have a chance to play in this playground.

By the time Tee asked me to write the story, I'd already gotten deeply into my own steampunk novel, *The Perils of Prague*. Since *Perils* was very much a story about technology and the uses that people put it to, I wanted to make this story different. After considering a few options, I decided to go for a creature story. And what creature is more iconically Scottish than the Loch Ness Monster? Then I figured, what is the point of having one creature when you can easily have two? After that, the story just needed a touch of magic for flavor.

I hope you enjoyed it.

THE BLESSING OF THE
CHEESE

FOREWORD

These next few stories are set in the world of *The Perils of Prague*, what I have been calling the World of the Eternal Empress. The first three have never before been in print, although this story has been heard. A little more about that later.

Before I even got started on the first draft of *Perils*, I'd already planned out the settings and story lines for the first six major adventures. While I was working on the book, I decided that in order to get a better feel for my world and my characters, whenever I was tempted to write a short story, I'd turn it into a Crackle and Bang adventure and set it somewhere along their travels.

The next four stories are Crackle and Bang Vignettes. Small stories set between the larger adventures. When you travel a lot, there are lots of opportunities along the way to discover something you never thought existed.

This first Crackle and Bang Vignette is… a little cheesy.

THE BLESSING OF THE CHEESE

"Up here, just a little farther!" Professor Crackle crowed as he pushed through the crowd of dusky Turks filling the narrow alley that passed for a street in this part of the city. Miss Bang followed in his wake, looking almost like one of the native women with a bright blue scarf wrapped about her head and tucked up to keep the dust out of her face. The professor stood out, as usual, with his twice begoggled top hat perched on his head. I hurried to keep up with them, my arms laden with a sloshing pot that kept threatening to spill its contents every time I was jostled by the crowd.

"Professor, why are we taking a tour of the slums of Constantinople?" I asked as another dark, unwashed resident pushed past me.

"Istanbul, my lord. You must not offend our Ottoman hosts by using the old name." Miss Bang's face was hidden by her scarf, but her eyes were clearly chiding me.

"Quite right. Besides, my boy, these aren't slums. This is the working class district. And we're here at the invitation of Mehmet Sadik. He's a sufi, a sort of local holy man. Should be right up here." He turned and pushed back into the mass of packed humanity.

Miss Bang took up the explanation. "Sufis are ascetics. They embrace a simple lifestyle in order to purify themselves and come closer to God. They are very respected in Ottoman society."

I sighed. "I understand we're paying respects to a local holy man. I don't understand *why* we are bringing him a pot of creamed corn." I hefted the aforementioned copper vessel up so Miss Bang was reminded of its presence.

She tilted her head slightly. "As a gift, naturally. One should always bring a gift when one goes calling." She took me by the arm and we pushed on after Professor Crackle.

"I know, but corn?"

"Corn is a delicacy in this part of the world. It isn't grown locally, so from Mr. Sadik's point of view this is an opportunity to try something very rare and special."

"But, did the professor have to have it creamed?"

"I believe Mr. Sadik requested that we bring something of a dairy nature, and this was Harmonious' solution." She looked over the heads of the locals. "I believe he has found the address." I followed her gaze and spotted the professor standing in front of an unassuming hut waving one arm frantically over his head.

We made our way through the crowd and joined the professor as he rapped on the door. The stained portal was whisked open to reveal a short thin man in a turban. He had a neatly trimmed beard, and was dressed simply in a white tunic and matching trousers. He blinked at us for a few moments before he recognized us and his eyes went wide and a huge smile spread over his face. "Hello! Hello, my friends! Come in, come in! Come and be welcome, my home greets you with great joy!"

He ushered us into the small hut that appeared to be a single large room. Shelves and a simple pantry were set against the far wall next to a small hearth. A low table occupied much of the room with cushions arrayed around it. In contrast to the dusty streets, everything inside was scrupulously clean. He closed the door behind us, shutting out the noise of the street.

Professor Crackle turned to the small man. "Thank you so much for inviting us, Mr. Sadik. It is a pleasure to meet you. I am Professor Harmonious Crackle. This is my colleague, Miss Titania Bang," Miss

Bang untucked the end of her scarf and greeted Mr. Sadik with a smile and a small bow. "And this…"

The small brown man grabbed my hand, cutting the professor off in the middle of his introduction. "Sir! Such a pleasure to meet you. Even here, in Istanbul, we have heard of your heroism in Prague!" He pumped my hand vigorously.

"It wasn't really that heroic, Mr. Sadik. I'm afraid the accounts are rather exaggerated."

"Ah! So modest! I am sure we will be fast friends! Please, call me Mehmet!" He grabbed my arms and for a second, I thought he was going to hug me. "Come, sit, sit. Oh, I am a horrible host! Please, make yourselves comfortable."

Professor Crackle took the pot from my hands. "We have brought you a gift, Mehmet. Something very rare in this part of the world: creamed corn." The professor removed the lid from the pot with a flourish.

If anything, Mr. Sadik's grin became wider. "Excellent, excellent! That will do nicely! Oh, this will be such a treat!"

The professor replaced the lid, placed the pot in the center of the small table, and we seated ourselves on the cushions grouped around the table. Mr. Sadik burst into a flurry of activity, pulling plates and food from the pantry, while keeping up a constant chatter. He served us thinly sliced sausages, a salad of mixed grains and spices, some odd-looking vegetables, and, of course, the corn. There were no utensils, but there was plenty of flat bread which we used for anything that wasn't a finger food. The professor and Miss Bang took to it as a matter of course, but my clumsy fingers made a mess of it and it was difficult for me to get a bite of anything without spilling some of it. Mr. Sadik proved to be a gracious host, telling me not to worry about my messes and all that mattered was that I enjoyed the food.

The food was quite tasty, although the flavors were unusual. Even the corn was surprisingly good. Mr. Sadik served us an excellent blend of strong dark tea in short, tulip-shaped glasses. He poured each glass from an odd double teapot that reminded me of a samovar.

When we finished eating, Professor Crackle turned to our host.

"Thank you for your hospitality, Mehmet, but I have to wonder, why did you invite us to join you in the first place?"

Our host nodded. "Yes, yes. When I heard that you were stopping over in Istanbul after that business in Bohemia, well, I knew that Allah meant for me to reach out to you. You are each persons of extraordinary circumstance. Allah has chosen you to do great things, and endure great hardships along your journey. As such, you can surely use all the blessings you can get. So, I have asked you here to bestow upon you the Blessing of the Cheese."

We blinked at him. He seemed entirely serious.

"But, you didn't serve any cheese," I said. At least, I didn't think anything he served was cheese.

Sadik rose in a single smooth motion and crossed to his pantry again. He lifted a cloth from a wedge of cheese on a plate, and broke off a small piece with his fingers. He returned to the table and dropped the fragment of cheese into the pot, stirring it into the remaining creamed corn before setting the serving spoon aside. Finally, he replaced the lid on the copper pot and dropped back down to his cushion. He beamed at us.

"I'm afraid I don't understand, Mehmet. What was the significance of that?" Professor Crackle gestured to the pot.

"A moment, my friend. The miracle cannot be rushed."

"Miracle?" Miss Bang asked, but appeared to ponder the situation.

We sat there in silence for several moments, not knowing what we were waiting for.

I noticed a slight motion on the table. "Um…" I looked, but didn't see anything out of the ordinary at first. And then I saw it.

The lid on the copper pot was slowly rising.

"Is it supposed to do that?"

Mr. Sadik patted my knee. "Patience, my friend. It is almost ready."

Professor Crackle bent low over the table. "This is fascinating, Mehmet. Is this a chemical reaction?"

"An extremely active biological culture?" Miss Bang suggested.

"One cannot analyze a miracle, good lady. One can only appreciate it for what it is."

The professor reached out for the lid of the pot, but Mr. Sadik stopped him. "Not yet, my friend."

The lid rose about an inch above the top of the pot, held aloft on a column of glossy white material. It shuddered for a second, and the column seemed to contract slightly.

"And it is done!" Mr. Sadik declared and removed the lid with a flourish, revealing a cylinder of pale white...

"Cheese?" I said.

"What else?" He rose again, grabbing a fresh plate from the pantry and a large knife. With practiced fingers, he lifted the fresh round of cheese from the pot, placing it on the plate and cutting it in half. He returned one half of the round to the pot and continued to cut slices off of the remaining portion. Once he had cut several slices, he distributed them to us. "Eat, my friends. Share the Blessing of the Cheese."

I lifted a slice and examined it. It appeared to be an ordinary slice of creamy, white cheese. It was soft enough to be pliable, but was otherwise an unremarkable slice of aged cheese.

The professor produced a loupe from his pocket and examined the cheese through it. "How do you age it so quickly?"

Miss Bang broke her piece into two pieces. "Cheese curds I could understand. Even a soft cheese. But a hard cheese in a few seconds? I can see why you call it a miracle, Mehmet." She took a small bite of one slice. "Oh!" A beatific smile crossed over Miss Bang's face, and a similar one appeared on Mr. Sadik's.

"Now you understand, good lady. The cheese blesses you. Please, my friends. Eat, eat." He gestured to the professor and myself to eat.

I sniffed at the cheese. It seemed safe. I popped the slice into my mouth.

As it hit my tongue, my mouth seemed to explode with flavor. The cheese was wonderfully savory and seemed to virtually melt on my tongue. Along with the flavor, a wave of peace swept through me. My muscles relaxed, and I felt two vertebrae in my back pop as they slid into a more comfortable alignment. A sigh escaped my lips.

Mr. Sadik smiled and nodded. Professor Crackle gave us both a curious look. He took a small bite of his slice. His eyebrows rose briefly as he tasted it. "A tasty variety, but other than the method of production, it doesn't seem that remarkable."

"You don't feel any different, Professor?"

"No, my boy, how should I feel?"

For the first time, Mr. Sadik frowned. "You did not receive the blessing?"

Miss Bang's brows pulled forward. "You didn't experience a feeling of peace and contentment, Harmonious?"

He shook his head. "No."

Mr. Sadik looked concerned. "This is most unusual. Perhaps you should try some more?" He offered the plate of sliced cheese to the professor.

Professor Crackle ate another slice, and shook his head. "I'm afraid I don't feel anything. Other than the pleasure of eating an excellent cheese."

Miss Bang gestured to him. "Perhaps, your condition is preventing you from getting the full effect, Harmonious?"

He looked at her thoughtfully. "I supposed that is a possibility, although I've never experienced, or rather not experienced, something like this before."

"I do not understand." Mr. Sadik looked at Miss Bang and the professor. "Professor Crackle is ill?"

"Not exactly, Mehmet. He isn't unwell, per se…"

Professor Crackle touched her lightly on the arm, and concluded, "Suffice it to say, Mehmet, that I have a condition that doesn't interfere with my everyday life, but it does have some unusual side effects. This would appear to be one of them."

"I am so sorry, Professor Crackle. I regret that you cannot share in the blessing."

I looked at the half round of cheese in the pot. Then at the slices Mr. Sadik had arrayed on the plate. "Professor?"

"Yes, old chap?"

"Where did the corn go?" I pointed to the cut surfaces of the cheese. "There was corn in the pot when Mr. Sadik did his trick. Now the corn is gone. There should be bits of it embedded in the cheese."

He picked up the half-round of cheese and examined it closely. "You're right, my boy. Very strange."

Miss Bang gestured to the pot. "Does this always happen, Mehmet?"

"Oh, yes. As long as there is even a tiny touch of dairy in the dish, all that is left is the blessed cheese." He took a slice himself, sighing as he ate it.

"That shouldn't be possible, should it?" I looked at another piece of the cheese.

"Normally, I'd say not." The professor tapped the round twice with his fingers. A dull thud resulted each time.

"Perhaps a particularly aggressive culture consumed the corn? Digested it along with everything else?" Miss Bang suggested. "We could run some tests…"

"Mehmet, would you mind terribly if we took some of this cheese with us? To run some experiments on?"

He shook his head. "It is for you. For all of you. To take with you, and bring you some measure of peace as you face the hardships that lay in your path. This is my gift to you. The reason I asked you to call."

The professor nodded. "Excellent! Thank you, Mehmet, this will give us a chance to investigate the rapid as well…"

I put a second slice into my mouth and felt another wave of peacefulness wash over me. "Professor, on second thought, I don't think I want to know. I think I can live with the mystery of mystic cheese."

"But aren't you curious, my boy?"

"Yes. No." I sighed. "I just figure that some questions are better left unsolved. I think magic cheese that makes you feel better certainly qualifies."

"There's no such thing as magic, my boy…" the professor started, but Miss Bang silenced him with a hand on his arm.

"He's right, Harmonious. Let it go." She turned to our host. "Thank you, Mehmet. We are very grateful for your gift."

He bowed in his seat. "It is my pleasure, good lady. Allah's blessings be upon you all."

"But just a few simple experiments…" the professor began again.

Miss Bang's grip tightened on his arm. "Let it go, Harmonious. You don't want to be rude to our host."

He put his hand over hers and winced. For a moment he looked like he was trying to pry her hand off, but then he subsided and patted it instead. "Yes, perhaps you're right. My apologies, Mehmet. My curiosity…Ah!" He sighed explosively as Miss Bang released his arm. He rubbed it nervously. "It sometimes runs away with me."

Mr. Sadik nodded. "I understand, Professor. I understand."

The end.

AFTERWORD

The Blessing of the Cheese is partially inspired by my friends August Grappin and Erin Kazmark. So, this one is their fault. Gus and Erin run a podcast called The Melting Potcast which is a venue for short stories. They put out various writing prompts during the year and encourage listeners to submit short stories for them to use on the podcast. I've been listening to The Melting Potcast for a while, and when *Perils* was published last year, I decided it was time for me to do a story for them.

At any given time, there are two open prompts that listeners can submit stories based on. At the time I decided to submit a story, the two open prompts were "Submit a story about some kind of mystic cheese." and "Where has the corn gone?" My brain, being the warped place that it is, immediately put those two concepts together, and I had a story.

Ironically, it took me considerably longer to choose my setting and do the cultural research for the story. One of the hallmarks of my Crackle and Bang stories is that they are steampunk, but they take place anywhere in the world EXCEPT England. English steampunk tales have been done to death. In a Crackle and Bang adventure, I want to explore what is going on in the rest of the world. And I want to do so in a way that will be enjoyable for someone who is from that culture. This means that even though I have a certain Victorian, British-centric lens that I'm looking at the world through, I need my characters to have a bit of a multi-cultural awareness, and I need to do the research to understand the environment, the traditions, and what is culturally important so I can represent it faithfully.

That's a big order for a little short story. But I do what I can. I dug into Turkish culture, and farther back into traditions of the Ottoman Empire. I researched the food, the different religious sects, and tried to pull out elements that gave the story an Ottoman flair. Hopefully, you like what I've done.

If you're interested, you can also listen to this story in episode 52 of The Melting Potcast at http://themeltingpotcast.com/the-melting-potcast/episode-52-main-ingredient-a-little-seasoning-mystery-meal.

BEFORE BREAKFAST

FOREWORD

This story actually started out as the first scene for the next Crackle and Bang adventure, *The Kindred of Kali*. I wrote this scene, and I was writing the following one when I realized I was starting too far away from the action of that book, and I skipped ahead.

But I kept this section, because it stands so well on its own, and it give an interesting insight into our narrator's unusual talents.

BEFORE BREAKFAST

"**P**ull!"

Cold winds bit into me, despite the thick leather coat I wore, as I watched the dark disk rise in a majestic arc over the metal plates of *The Argos*. I grunted softly as I lifted the shotgun to my shoulder and sighted along the barrel at the dwindling clay pigeon. I let out my breath slowly as my finger tightened on the trigger, feeling the tension in the mechanism. Choosing my moment, I squeezed the trigger gently, the weapon booming and kicking back against my shoulder. I took the shock and continued to watch the clay pigeon as it sailed out of sight over the edge of the ship.

"Damn," I grumbled.

"I'm not sure I would have believed it if I hadn't seen it with my own eyes, my lord," Miss Bang shook her head as she gingerly took the shotgun from my hands. "I expected you to at least hit one of the pigeons."

"Yer bloody awful," added Tinka as she loaded another disk into the apparatus that launched the clay pigeon to its doom thousands of feet below us. "I can't believe you missed a whole dozen. Yer' a flippin' menace with a gun." She squatted next to a spring loaded trap mounted to the hull. A part of me wanted to argue with the four-armed engineer, if only to salve my pride. Unfortunately, the rest of me feared that she was right.

"Now, Tinka," Miss Bang admonished. "The shotgun simply isn't Sir Richard's weapon."

I nodded my head in appreciation of Miss Bang's explanation, but Tinka wasn't quite done with me yet.

"Are ye daft, Tanya? I've seen them what has never held a gun afore pop off two or three with a shotgun. He missed twelve! You don't get much worse than that!" She pointed at me with her upper left hand to punctuate her point.

"But he hasn't hit either of us, or the ship, so he isn't exactly a menace."

"So kind of you, Miss Bang. Perhaps we should call an end to this experiment?" I suggested, clinging to the little scraps of my dignity.

Instead of answering, Miss Bang gracefully bent and stowed the shotgun in the case at her feet. I looked past her toward the bow of *the Argos*. Past the gently curving slope of the airship's hull, I could see row after row of clouds, but as yet, no trace of the desert lands we were passing over. While the sands below were burning hot, at the altitude *the Argos* flew, the winds were still cold and biting. For that matter, the clouds were still few and far between, but at the angle we were seeing them, they appeared to be stacked up upon each other. Of course, from our position on top of the ship, we couldn't really see down to the desert without moving dangerously close to the edge. But while the lounges and balconies available below decks provided a better vantage point to the lands below, they weren't ideal for Miss Bang's firearms experiment.

She stood up again, pulling a rifle out of a second case. "I think it is time to move on to the second stage, my lord." I took the weapon from her with a sigh, and loaded cartridges into the ammunition port on the side.

"Isn't it harder to hit skeet with a rifle?" I asked as I pushed rounds into the weapon. "I'm not really sure what you're expecting to discover with this experiment, Miss Bang."

"I won't say it is impossible, as I have known a number of marksmen who were capable of it. But I have a suspicion that the normal rules may not apply to you, Sir Richard. You did display an uncanny ability with a pistol back in Prague, despite the fact that you'd never fired one before. These trials are merely to determine your level of skill with firearms, and determine if you have a general or specific talent in their use."

"Or if it was just a case of beginner's luck."

"That is one possibility, my lord." Tinka snorted in response to Miss Bang's comment.

I hefted the rifle. "Then I guess we had best get this over with."

Miss Bang nodded approvingly. "Tinka, Pull!"

I fared better with the rifle. I managed to clip the pigeons three times out of a dozen, which honestly surprised me given how poorly I had fared with the shotgun. I had used a rifle before for hunting, though not often. Yet, this time it felt different. It felt wrong. The gun was too big, too bulky somehow. It seemed like I was throwing around a cannon.

Miss Bang took the rifle back, and handed me a holstered pistol. I stripped the holster from the gun and tucked it into one of my pockets. The gun was a .22 caliber revolver ideal for target shooting. I loaded the gun, and pointed it to the deck, away from my companions. "You realize that the odds are that I'm going to miss every shot with this thing. A pistol doesn't have nearly the range of a rifle or a shotgun. It just isn't that accurate over that distance."

"Yes, my lord, but I still believe it is worth trying. Regardless of the outcome, we may still learn something useful from the attempt."

I raised the pistol. "Very well."

Miss Bang gave the command, and Tinka let the pigeon fly. The pistol leapt forward, but seemed off-balance in my hand. I fired without thinking, without even trying to aim, and saw the skeet change direction slightly. I dropped my weapon to a neutral position.

"Did I hit it?"

"I'm not sure, my lord," Miss Bang said. "Something happened, but it could have been a fault in the skeet. Shall we try again?"

Tinka launched the next skeet, which flew apart as my pistol let out a satisfying crack. Something still seemed off, but I was beginning to compensate for it.

"I don't believe it," Tinka whispered.

"Well done, my lord!" Miss Bang called over the wind.

"Thank you. Something still feels off balance, though. But I think I'm getting the hang of it."

"Really? Can I make a suggestion? In Prague, you drew your gun and fired without thinking. Everything else you did went from there. Perhaps we need to recreate that situation? Try putting on the holster and drawing from it when Tinka launches the skeet. Tinka, another pigeon, please." I returned the pistol to the holster, and attached it to my belt as Tinka deftly re-cocked the launcher and loaded a new skeet. Her extra pair of arms made her extremely efficient at the task. I made considerably less progress, as the cold wind cut into me as I had to open my coat and jacket to secure the holster to my belt. The temperature had already made my fingers a little stiff and clumsy. After a few minutes of fumbling I had the holster attached and tied down to my leg. I shook my hands out to try and force the blood back into them.

"Pull," cried Miss Bang.

Surprised, I reached for my gun as Tinka launched the skeet into the air. I watched the spinning clay disc as my hand snaked under my coat, and withdrew with the revolver held gently in my fingers. The gun felt light in my grasp. It fairly floated up in front of me as my eyes followed the pigeon. The pistol barked, and then dropped as fragments of clay scattered into the air. My hand snaked back up under my coat and stopped as the gun slid firmly back into its holster.

For several seconds, the only sound was that of the wind across the body of *the Argos*.

Tinka broke that silence. "Bloody hell!"

"Tinka, Language!"

She was unfazed at Miss Bang's rebuke. "Did you see that? Even with the bloody coat, the gun practically jumped into his hand. It was like he didn't have any bones! And he hit it!" She turned to me. "You hit it like it was just sitting there."

"I know. It just… felt right." I shrugged.

"It would seem that the pistol is very much your weapon, my lord."

Tinka scrambled to reload the trap. "Do it again!" Without waiting, she launched the freshly loaded pigeon.

The revolver slid effortlessly out of the holster and flickered upward with another report. The target exploded into fragments.

"Yes!" Tinka crowed.

"You do seem to have a natural talent with handguns, Sir Richard. Do you think you might be up to trying something a little more difficult?"

"I could certainly try. What did you have in mind?"

"Do you think you could try to hit the pigeon more than once?" Her head tilted to one side as she waited for my answer.

"I don't see how that is possible. Won't the pigeon shatter from the first hit? How can I hit it again?"

She pulled the edges of her fur coat tighter around her. "I was thinking about your first shot. If you didn't miss, but instead clipped the edge of the clay pigeon, that would make it change direction without shattering. Part of it would break off, naturally, but there ought to be a larger portion that you could aim at for a second shot."

"That sounds like an impossible shot," I said, "but I seem to be using that word a lot, and we already seem to be in that territory... so I guess I might was well try."

Tinka reset the trap as I reloaded the revolver, pocketing the spent brass and picking out the loaded cartridge. Fortunately, she waited for me before launching the skeet again. I opened my coat and pushed the right side of the fleece lined leather back to clear the holster.

"Very well, Pull."

The pigeon leapt from the trap and my arm lashed out. The gun barked and the skeet jumped in the air, shooting off in a new direction. My arm twitched again with another retort, and the skeet split again. A third retort sounded, but the pigeon had already broken apart, and the shot missed.

Tinka let out a prolonged howl, her arms raised in the air above her head. Miss Bang stood with a shocked look on her face. I couldn't believe it myself.

"Well," Miss Bang said at last, "I believe we have achieved our quota of impossible things for the morning. Shall we go down to breakfast?"

"Not yet, Miss Bang," I said, holding out a hand. "Tinka, please load the trap. I want to try that again."

She loaded the trap with a fresh clay pigeon, then looked up at me with a grin.

"Pull."

The final clay disc spun out over the metal plates of *the Argos*. The world seem to come to a crawl. I could see the faint wobble as the uneven pigeon sped away from me. The wind quieted, and seem to slow, as if it had been removed to a distance. I never even felt my arm move. Suddenly, the pistol was in front of me. Bang. The pigeon leapt up and to the left. Bang. It jumped up again, this time speeding to the right. Bang. The clay pigeon shattered, minute particles spreading out in all directions and then being whisked away as the wind returned and the world resumed its normal pace.

I restored the pistol to its holster, and buttoned up my coat.

The two of them were mute with disbelief as they stared where moments ago the skeet had danced across the sky.

"Ladies, I believe you said something about breakfast?"

AFTERWORD

I love this story for two reasons.

The first is an Alice Through the Looking-Glass callback to believing six impossible things before breakfast.

The second is that when I was editing *Perils* I found that His Lordship very frequently declared that things were impossible. Upwards of half a dozen times! I had to cut the number down in the editing, because he's dim but not THAT dim. After declaring something as impossible three or four times and being proven wrong EVERY TIME, even he begins to twig to the idea that he's using the wrong word.

So, how much fun would it be to take that doubting character and have him find out that he can actually DO something impossible? Lots!

Also, how often do I get to get to have Tinka jeer, cheer, and be left speechless by the same person?

MARKET DAY

FOREWORD

This is also an original tale written for this collection.

After looking at my character's progress from Prague to Istanbul, and taking a peek at their destination in India for *Kindred* (No spoilers!), I looked at the map and tried to figure out if there was a good place on the map that was right about in the middle of their journey that would make an excellent place to stop and look around. And there it was. Tehran.

Now, in our world, Tehran isn't the most welcoming spot for a lot of people. But in the World of the Eternal Empress, things happened a bit differently. When unrest occurred in nations around the world, The Empress issued an edict to world rulers: "Keep the peace, or I will keep it for you." It was quickly discovered that keeping the peace meant making the people happy, not crushing resistance under your heel. Those who made the mistake of oppressing their people soon found their country had been annexed by the empire. Wise rulers quickly learned that it was in their best interest to take their people's complaints seriously.

So in the World of the Eternal Empress, the Shah of Iran listened to his people. He cut back on some of the excesses of the ruling class, and adopted a number of popular reforms. This blunted some of the growing religious fervor in Iran, and allowed him to stay in power, although he's still walking a tightrope.

But for our characters, this means that Iran has an unusual blend of old world charm and modern civic planning. A garden spot. As long as you don't break the law…

MARKET DAY

The Persian market was not what I expected.

Our previous stop in Istanbul had left me with an impression of Eastern markets as being dusty, crowded places. Endless rows of tents packed full of unwashed humanity. Miss Bang insisted that what little we had seen was only one of the poorer examples of what the Turks had to offer, and that many markets were in fact full of wonders beyond imagination.

As we ventured into the Grand Bazaar of Tehran, I began to think that she was correct.

With each breath, new aromas tantalized my senses. Exotic spices. Savory meats. The scents of breads and pastries, freshly baked, tickled my nose. The streets were lined with colorful stalls. This one filled with piles of fruits and vegetables, the next overflowing with a variety of flowers. Other stalls held pans of spices in a riot of hues, or were draped with textiles in a variety of patterns and fabrics. Banners strung between the stalls fluttered in the breeze.

The people were colorful as well. Men in brightly colored robes, or livery. Women draped in silks and other diaphanous fabrics in styles that ranged from shapeless outfits that covered almost every inch of skin, to eye-catching outfits that were little more than a handful of artfully placed veils. The few westerners in their khaki outfits looked drab in comparison to the locals.

My tan linen suit was not the height of fashion, but it breathed well enough to keep me from overheating under the Persian sun. A wide-brimmed felt hat kept the sun out of my eyes. In contrast, Professor Crackle shaded his eyes with one hand held up to the brim of his customary top hat adorned with two pairs of goggles strapped around it. He should have been roasting in the thick wool frock coat he wore over his green paisley waistcoat, but he showed no signs of feeling the heat. Miss Bang, as usual, was a vision in a yellow day dress with a matching silk veil. She remained cool and collected as she shopped among the stalls of the wide market lane.

"So, why are we stopping here, Professor?" I asked as we waited while Miss Bang haggled in a fluid tongue with a vendor of fruits and vegetables. "I thought *the Argos* was well stocked for a much longer journey."

"Oh, it is, it is, my boy. I had originally planned to fly straight through to India, but the last few days I've felt the urge to stretch my legs, as it were." He blinked at me through his wire rimmed glasses. "You know how it is. No matter how comfortable your surroundings, after a while you just yearn for something new. Besides, Tehran was right along our course and represented an excellent opportunity to stock some local produce. And it is such a beautiful city!'

I had to agree with the professor on that score. The city was filled with spires and minarets covered with amazing tile work tracing out intricate geometric designs. Surprisingly lush parks and gardens dotted the landscape. And then there was the Shah's palace. It was beautiful from the ground, and positively stunning from the air. We weren't permitted to bring *the Argos* too close to the palace, but the view was remarkable.

Miss Bang passed a handful of coins to the merchant. He bowed as he received the coins, and passed a small bag back to Miss Bang. As she turned away, the vendor shouted out orders to his assistants who scrambled about assembling packets of produce. She stepped up to us, plucking a wizened-looking date from the bag and biting it in half.

"Mmmmm," she purred as she chewed. "These dates are delicious.

Do try one, my lord, Harmonious." She proffered the bag to us as she popped the other half in her mouth and savored it.

"Thank you, my dear," the professor replied as he plunged his hand into the bag and claimed his prize.

Miss Bang held the bag out to me. "My lord?"

I eyed the somewhat crumpled bag a bit dubiously. "I, uh, I'm afraid I've never had dates before."

"Oh, you simply must try one, my lord. They're delightfully sweet. I'm sure you'll love it."

I looked over the edge of the bag at the brown, slightly glistening mass within. "Are you sure?"

She laughed. "It's only a date, my lord. Just candied fruit. It won't hurt you." She proffered the bag again.

I sighed and reached a tentative finger and thumb into the bag. The shiny surface proved to be a gummy, sticky substance that covered the dates, making them stick together. I managed to separate a single item from the rest and pulled it from the mass only to find a second squishy brown oval was stuck to the sad looking fruit I had extracted.

"Bon appetit!" Miss Bang said, and then turned to join the professor as he wandered down the line of shops.

The two congealed dates sticking to my fingers were about as far from a delectable foodstuff as I could imagine. The gooey shapes looked more like something I would try to scrape off of my shoe than something I would put into my mouth. I tried to convince myself they must be safe, as my companions had eaten them without hesitation, but a small voice in the back of my head reminded me that they were both considerably more worldly than I. There was no telling what bizarre foods they had learned to eat in their travels.

I had resolved instead to simply discard the fruits and rejoin my companions when I became aware of the grocer from the nearby stall looking at me and smiling. He nodded and grinned, encouraging me with a wave of his right hand. He said something in his native tongue that I couldn't understand, and then followed it up with broken English. "Good dates. Good dates." Again he waved his hand.

Unable to discard the problem foodstuff, I smiled back and raised the sticky mass to him in a small salute. I now had no choice but to consume them. I took a small bite of the squishy substance. It was chewy and oddly tough, but powerfully sweet as well. I chewed carefully, unsure of what I was eating. The fruit was unexpectedly fibrous as I ground it between my teeth. There was also an unusual savory flavor to it that seemed familiar, but I couldn't quite place. I went to take another bite, and found myself sucking the sticky syrup off of my fingers, the dates themselves having been efficiently consumed.

The grocer gave a laugh. "See. Good dates!" I tipped my hat to him and hurried after my companions, feeling somewhat like a small child who had been caught with his hand in the cookie jar. But, I still wouldn't say no if Miss Bang offered me another date.

I dodged past a knot of shoppers and caught up to Professor Crackle and Miss Bang as they stopped to admire the wares of a local rug merchant. The stall was covered with an assortment of rugs in various sizes, from small prayer rugs up to a large floor rug that was rolled out on the street in front of the booth. Each rug was covered in intricate patterns of bright colors.

As I approached, a large, bearded man stepped out of the booth. He spread his hands wide in a gesture of welcome as he called out to us. "A most discerning eye you have, my friends! And one that knows quality, too, for it has brought you to Farkoosh's humble booth. What may I show you, good gentiles? I have rugs from the finest looms in all Iran! A souvenir of your trip abroad, perhaps? Not a prayer rug, I think. You do not look the type. A runner perhaps? An entry rug? Something larger? Name your desire, my friends, and if I do not have it, I shall find it. I have a variety of marvels at my command." He smiled broadly.

"Actually, I was admiring this remarkable specimen you have here," the professor said and gestured to the large rug spread upon the cobblestones.

"Ah, now that, that is a very special rug. It was woven in antiquity, but shows no sign of age. Each fiber is as fresh and strong as the day it was cut from the loom. But more than that, there is power in this rug, and it obeys the will of its master. Behold!" He stood next to the rug, his hands thrust out as if he was grabbing it by the edges, strain showing in his fingers as he intoned. His words made no sense to me, but his tone sounded dark, mysterious, and intense.

The rug leapt into the air, and calmly floated a foot off of the ground.

"Fascinating!" the professor exclaimed and stepped · forward to examine the rug more closely, but instead his feet shot out from under him and he tumbled to the ground.

I stepped forward to help the professor back to his feet, but the surface proved to be impossibly slick, and lost my balance and crumpled to the ground next to him. We tried to regain our feet, but no matter how we turned, Professor Crackle and I were unable to gain a purchase to right ourselves.

"Harmonious, Sir Richard, wait!" Miss Bang called to us, bringing a halt to our struggles. We looked at her as she stood nearby, and she directed our gaze to the hem of her skirt. Her shoes were clearly visible to us, as the hem of her dress on the side nearest us now floated about a foot above the street, dropping off to its accustomed length as it got farther from us. She stepped back from us and the fabric dipped as if it slid off the surface of a table. She stepped forward and as the edge of her skirt swung forward, it floated back up in the air again, gaining no more than a foot in height.

"How...?" I began, but the professor interrupted me.

"Of course! Magnetic repulsion! I should have known."

"I'm sorry, Professor?" I turned to him, but he crawled past me to Miss Bang's side and was able to stand up again.

The merchant continued his pitch. "No need to abase yourselves, my friends. While this is indeed a genuine magical carpet, and to some priceless beyond measure, Farkoosh has other offerings more marvelous still!"

"Poppycock!" retorted Professor Crackle. "There's no such thing as magic, my good man, only scientific principles disguised with clever trickery." I shuffled aside until my feet regained traction once more. Miss Bang appeared at my side and helped me up. The merchant sputtered as the professor continued. "Now, I'll give you credit, this one was very cleverly disguised. You must have wires woven into the fabric of the carpet, and a matrix of some sort buried under the cobblestones. You say a bit of blather and some accomplice in the back flips a switch and the whole thing rises. Rather well done, if I must say so."

"So, why did the ground become slick, Professor?"

Miss Bang supplied the explanation. "The ground didn't become slick, my lord. Indeed, for just about anyone else, there wouldn't have been a noticeable difference. But, you remember, our shoes have metal plates in them. Repeated use of *the Argos'* lift will have given them a slight magnetic charge, one which is apparently repelled by the field this gentlemen is using to deceive unsuspecting tourists. It seemed slippery because your feet never touched the ground. They slid across the air, buoyed up by the magnetic field."

The shopkeeper protested his innocence, claiming to be a simple purveyor of fine goods, but the professor simply talked over him. "A rather strong field. It would have to be to lift up two grown men. The power requirements would be phenomenal." The merchant raised his volume as the professor continued. "I'm surprised we can't hear a generator right now. They've either hidden a considerable length of cable, or the generator is nearby but remarkably well soundproofed." Falling to his knees, the rug vendor grabbed his robes and began screaming about the injustice of the false accusations being lain upon him by the professor. "Then again perhaps we could find it if it wasn't for all this noise! Would you please pipe down, sir! We are not deceived, but if you continue making so much racket, I fear we may have no choice but to alert the local constabulary!"

"Stop! Thief!" a voice called out from behind us. We turned to see a dirty boy clutching several flat loaves of bread dodging through the shoppers. Chasing him was a man wearing an apron and covered in flour across his chest and up both arms. The boy made straight for us, and I leaned in to grab him, but my feet were suddenly swept out from under me again.

The child surged past the professor and I as we fell to the ground. Even Miss Bang tumbled to the ground before rolling to her feet several strides away from us. The urchin leapt onto the floating carpet with his spoils, and the carpet promptly reared up and sped through the market, its occupant deftly steering it around the dodging pedestrians by leaning one way or the other.

The baker staggered to a panting halt next to us, and we must have been a sight. Five faces, the rug merchant included, watching open-mouthed as the thief made good his escape atop a flying carpet.

Miss Bang translated for the baker, who only spoke a smattering of English. "His name is Yousef. He says he has been tending his shop alone since his wife was killed and his daughter stolen away. This made him a target for the local urchins. They steal the bread for food, but since he must bake and tend the shop, he cannot make enough to cover the losses. He has tried to hire assistants, but the work is too hard for them. They run away." She lowered her voice. "Harmonious, he is a kind man. He doesn't fault the children for trying to survive, but his business if failing. He just wants the stealing to stop."

"Yes. Yes, I daresay he does. I don't blame him." Professor Crackle lifted his eyes from the dirt he had been poking around in. "It seems that we shall need to track down this thief, then. And I hope find out just how he was able to make good his escape."

"Isn't sailing away on a magic carpet good enough, Professor?" I asked.

He looked at me over his glasses. "A *fake* magic carpet, my friend."

The rug vendor's back straightened and he shot the professor a hot look. "Sir, do not impugn my wares! I sell only the finest…"

"Fake magic carpets," the professor finished for him. "Oh, do stop pretending man. We both know there is no such thing as magic, and how you did the levitating trick. The point is that as soon as that child pushed the carpet off of your magnetic field, it should have crashed to the ground. It didn't. Something the boy did kept it aloft. But what?"

"Another magnetic field, Harmonious?" Miss Bang eyed the street the carpet had fled down.

"Undoubtedly. But the larger the field, the higher the power demands. The child would never have been able to generate or steal enough power to create a magnetic field over half this street, much less all the side ways and alleys that he would have needed in order to be assured of his escape."

I rubbed my head. "But why would he need such a large field, Professor? All he really needs is to keep the carpet aloft."

"That's just it, my boy. He needs to keep the carpet on top of the magnetic field to keep it aloft."

"No, Harmonious! If the carpet is generating the magnetic field, it will move with him." Miss Bang grabbed the professor's arm. "That would only require a fraction of the power to lift the carpet and the boy's weight. All he would need would be enough metal underneath him to push off against." She looked at me. "Brilliant, my lord."

"I'll take your word for it, Miss Bang, as I've no idea what you've just said."

"It seems unlikely to me." Professor Crackle sounded skeptical. "The boy would have to carry his own power system. A generator would be too conspicuous, so it would have to be a battery of some kind. But surely that would make the apparatus too heavy for him to move, much less run with it."

"I don't know, Harmonious." Miss Bang tapped a finger against her lips. "The weight would be a problem, but I don't think it would be insurmountable." Her eyes suddenly got wide. "Especially if it was supplemented by an external power source."

The professor looked at Miss Bang, pushing his top hat back on his head. "What are you thinking, my dear? You've obviously got something in mind."

"What if instead of a single magnetic field, our thief used two weaker fields: one on the carpet, and on the street, both with the same polarity so they repel each other and the carpet would slide over it."

I looked at the baker and the rug merchant, but neither of them were following the conversation either.

Professor Crackle grasped Miss Bang's hands. "Yes! That could work. And if he had an accomplice switching the power between different streets, then it could be managed with even less power. Genius!"

"Does this give us a way of tracking our thief, Professor?" I didn't see much use in figuring out how the trick was done if it meant that our culprit still made a clean getaway.

The professor turned to face me, but his eyes looked through me.

They danced left to right as he considered the question. "Yes. Yes, I think it does. If Miss Bang is correct, there should be a network of metal plates laid into the street, and they should be wired together. We ought to be able to follow them back to wherever our thief went."

I looked at the cobblestoned street. The hard stones were set close together and were quite level. There was no sign that any of them had been disturbed. "It doesn't look like anything has been disturbed, Professor. How could someone lay metal plates under the street?"

"Not under, my boy. In!" The professor dug into his pockets and pulled out his new harmonic spanner. He fitted it with a tuning fork and struck it against the cobbles. As the tones rang out from the device, we gathered a number of stares from other shoppers. I waved somewhat nervously at them, and after a moment that seemed to satisfy them that we weren't up to anything nefarious, or worthy of their interest. When I turned back to my companions, Miss Bang and the baker were intently following what the professor was doing as he directed his harmonic spanner at the street. The rug merchant look at me and declared, "This has nothing to do with me. I have a shop to attend to." He slowly backed away with his hands raised in front of him. When I didn't challenge him, he scuttled away and dove back into his booth.

I looked back to the professor to find him tuning his harmonic spanner as he pointed it at a crack between two of the cobblestones. As he shifted it to a higher frequency, I could hear a rattling. The professor became increasingly excited as he narrowed in on the source. As I watched, a thin slip of metal vibrated up from between the cobbles. The professor plucked at it with eager fingers and pried it from between the stones. He lifted it, and I could see that it was a small, oddly shaped flat piece of metal with thin wires trailing from it at two different ends.

"Ah, see! See!" He pulled on the wires, unearthing them from the cracks between the stones. "Plates connected together by wires. This is how he was able to generate enough of a magnetic field to escape. This is amazing. It's made of scrap. Just odds and ends put together in a technical hodgepodge. Absolutely fascinating!"

"This is how, we find... thief?" the baker asked in halting English.

"Yes, yes," the professor answered. "We follow the wire, and it should take us where he went. When it was apparent that he didn't understand, Miss Bang translated for him.

Yousef nodded. "Then, I go with."

"That's not necessary, my good man. We will find your thief. Never fear." Professor Crackle smiled up at the larger man.

"I go with," he repeated.

"I don't think he's going to take no for an answer, Professor." I looked up at the muscular baker. "And it might be handy to have him along in case we run into trouble."

"I believe Sir Richard has a point, Harmonious. We've already speculated that our quarry may not be working alone. If he has allies, we may need Yousef's assistance."

He looked at Miss Bang and then back to the baker. Returning his gaze to Miss Bang, he said, "I think you may have a point." He nodded. "Very well, young man, come along. It is going to be a bit of work to trace these wires back to their source and our quarry already has a head start."

We proceeded to spend the next couple hours prying wires and metal plates from the streets as we worked our way. I garnered a number of strange looks as I trailed along behind my companions carrying a slowly growing ball of wire and scrap. Some pulled from the ground easily, while other pieces had to be pried loose by the professor's harmonic device. The plates, as the professor had noted, were bits of scrap. Some were already flat pieces of metal, while others had been pounded flat, or nearly so. Even the wires joining the pieces together were salvaged from something else. Bits of wire twisted together, or just long strips of thin metal bent into shape to fit between the cracks in the street.

The trail of wires led us down the streets of the market, but quickly branched off into less reputable side streets. There were other wires crossing the path we followed, but most of those proved to be cross pieces connecting parallel strands into a network across the street.

Others proved to lead down smaller side streets, and several times we found ourselves forced to backtrack as they proved to be dead ends.

As the afternoon waned, we found ourselves following the trail of scrap and wires into an increasingly disreputable neighborhood next to a power station. The professor surmised that the power was most likely stolen from the station. There weren't many people in the neighborhood, as it appeared to be mostly warehouses and abandoned stores.

We came across the missing carpet rolled up next to a warehouse that looked like it had been vacant for a number of years. Or perhaps mostly vacant would be a better term?

"Professor," I asked as I dropped the armful of wire and scrap metal next to the carpet, "Wouldn't caution be the better point of valor at this juncture? We've been expecting the boy to have accomplices. If there are a number of them, we might be in trouble."

He nodded energetically. "Quite right. Quite right, my boy. From here on stealth shall be our watchword. No unnecessary noise. All of us must keep our voices down."

"Thief!" the baker bellowed at the top of his lungs. "I have tracked you to your lair! I will have you now, thief!" He stormed into the abandoned warehouse, repeating his challenge in his native language.

"Or not," added Professor Crackle as he and Miss Bang followed the Persian man into the building.

I sighed. "One of these days you'd think I'd learn to keep my mouth shut." I eyed the broken door that my companions had just entered through, then spared a glance at the deserted street and the other disheveled buildings around me. "And it looks like today will not be the day, either." I said to myself as I entered the ruined structure.

I stopped just inside the door to allow my eyes to adjust to the dim interior. The baker's shouts echoed off the walls were muffled, indicating that the structure wasn't entirely empty. The professor was about a dozen paces ahead of me, trying to calm the man without much success. Faint shafts of light peeked in through broken shutters placed high on the building's walls. I blinked my eyes to help them adapt.

The first impression I had was of piles of rubbish stacked up to either side of me. I blinked again and realized that they were actually shelves on either side of the entrance that had been piled to overflowing with scavenged items, and had larger items leaned against them, forming a makeshift bulwark. Other piles dotted the floor, or were stacked on similar shelves that stood in broken rows around the building. These didn't appear to be defensive structures, like the ones I stood next to, but instead resembled large nests. A few tables dotted the open areas of the floor, some with broken legs propped up on other debris. A single large table dominated the center of the largest open area. It was piled with odd bits of scrap, what looked to be partially assembled machines. It resembled a messy version of one of the professor's work benches.

Yousef and Professor Crackle stood in front of the large bench, the Persian man looking to the stacks and shelves, while the professor peered through the dimness at the equipment on the tables before him. Miss Bang was no where to be seen.

"Come out, boy!" the baker roared. "You must stop stealing from my shop. You are driving me to ruin. If I lose my shop, what will you do then, eh? What will you do when there is no bread to steal?"

The professor patted his hands in the air while still peering at the items on the bench. "Now, there is no need for that, my good man. No need for anyone to go out of business, or to go hungry." He picked up one of the trinkets in front of him. "These are very good. Excellent design, especially given the crude materials you've had to work with." He turned, addressing the shadows of the warehouse. "You've no need to steal, my boy. With this kind of skill you could easily earn money by selling these devices. You've no need to steal. Let us help you."

A youthful voice replied from the shadows. "You know nothing. No one will trade fairly with us. They do not see us, or if they do, they beat us to drive us away. Our families abandoned us. There is no other life for aaaAAAgh!" The voice cut off and I could hear sounds of struggle in the darkness. Other sounds of scurrying feet erupted all

over the warehouse. A confusion of sound made it impossible to determine where the struggle was happening. Two small figures appeared
out of the walls next to me and tried to rush past me out of the building. They were surprised when I grabbed them around the middle and
picked them up. They struggled wildly, kicking and biting, but it was
the stench of them that nearly overwhelmed me. They stank of sweat
and dirt and filth, and the waves of odor coming off of them as they
fought made my eyes water.

A line of sparks shot across the ceiling of the warehouse and light
flooded the room, blinding me, now that my eyes had acclimated to
the dark. I threw the two struggling urchins back into the middle of the
room and blinked again to clear my eyes before setting my feet for
them to try to rush me again. Instead, when they hit the floor, they
immediately scrambled for the walls and hid in the piles of debris. The
room was bathed in light from a dozen lamps, all different, that hung
between a pair of sparking wires. All sounds of movement stopped
and it was quiet once more.

Miss Bang stepped out from behind one of the sets of shelves,
pushing a small figure clad in rags ahead of her. It was the bread thief
we had seen earlier in the market.

"There you are, thief!" The baker strode over to them, Professor
Crackle close behind.

"Harmonious, I think we've run into a bit of a complication," Miss
Bang said, and quietly pulled the ragged turban from the boy's head,
revealing locks of long, dark hair.

"It's a girl!" the professor blurted out. "Well done, young miss! This
is remarkable work, you should be very proud. How did you manage
to build such a powerful portable charging system? And how did you
overcome the weight limitations?"

"Professor!" I called out.

"It's a perfectly valid question!"

"Not what I meant." I pointed to the baker.

Yousef's face had changed when Miss Bang pulled the turban off
of the child. The anger had drained from it and was replaced by a
strange wonder. He seemed both confused and in awe at the same
time. He moved slowly towards the girl, going down on his knees.

He stretched one hand out to her. "Farzanah? Daughter? Is it truly you?"

The girl pushed back into Miss Bang's skirts, shying away from his outstretched hand.

"Farzanah," he repeated plaintively, "why did you not come home?"

"Why did you not look for me, Father?" the girl spat back at him. "When the men grabbed Mother, I ran and ran. I was lost. Why did you not find me, Father? Why did you not look for me?"

The baker sunk to the floor. Tears welled up in his eyes. "I did. I looked for you for months! I thought you had been taken by the same men who killed your mother. I thought they had killed you too. I would have given anything to know that you were alive. My only wish has been to have you back with me." He swallowed back a sob. "But now, now we have found each other again. Now you can come home. We can be a family again." He gazed hopefully up at his daughter.

She narrowed her eyes and glared at her father. He gave her a pleading look in return, and her gaze softened a bit. "I am sorry, father, but I cannot go with you. They need me here. They took me in when I had nothing, and I will not abandon them."

The baker blinked. The professor took a step toward her and said in a gentle tone, "But you can go home, my dear. You don't have to live like this anymore."

The girl spared him a glance. I thought at first that she was about eight years old, but hearing her talk, seeing how she behaved, I'd adjusted my guess upward. It was obvious the streets had aged her before her time. But judging from the look that she gave the professor, I'd say she was twelve going on forty. However young she was, she meant business.

"And how will they live if I am gone? Who will protect them? If I go, they all come with me. All."

"Um…" I interjected. "How many people are we talking about?" The others looked at me as if they had forgotten I was there. Which I suppose they had.

The girl barked a command in her native language. For a moment, nothing happened. She repeated the command and made a collecting motion with her left hand. All around the room over a dozen children suddenly appeared. They stepped out of piles of rubbish or popped up out of the floor or walls. All were ragged and dirty, of course. They appeared to range in age from 4 to 10 years, and looked about half starved.

The girl, Farzanah, took a step forward, Miss Bang still maintaining a grip on her shoulder. "What will it be, Father? None or all? Will you have no children, or fifteen?"

The baker looked around the room, finding the faces of each of the children as they stared back at him, their faces like masks, giving nothing away. Tears were streaming down his face as he turned back to Miss Bang and his daughter. "To have the light back in my life? To have a home filled with the laughter of children? To teach my work to sons and daughters? For that, I will give everything. If you will not come with me, then I will stay with you. I will take all."

"Truly, Father?"

"I swear to you, Farzanah, by the love I have for your mother, and under the light of Allah, I will take these children to be my own and raise them in love from this day until I breathe my last." He spread his arms wide. "May Allah strike me down if I do not."

The girl bit her lip for a minute, then slipped from Miss Bang's grasp and rushed into his arms. He enfolded her in his arms, murmuring, "Oh, light of my eyes, I had never thought to hold you again. I am blessed this day." His words became muffled as he buried his face in the girl's hair. They hugged and cried for about a minute, swaying back and forth. The first one to move was a small boy whom I took to be about five years old. He sprang from one of the nests on the floor and dashed over to throw his arms around the two of them. This started the flood, as children pounded across the warehouse floor and wrapped themselves around Yousef. Miss Bang and the professor came to join me by the door.

"Well, I'd say that was a successful conclusion to that mystery, eh?" The professor rubbed his hands together.

"I would say so," Miss Bang replied. Her eyes also looked a bit misty.

"So, my boy, while we're waiting for them to get reacquainted, do come give me a hand rolling up that carpet outside."

I looked at him in disbelief. "You're not planning on giving it back to that crooked rug vendor, are you Professor? He uses it to swindle people!"

Professor Crackle shook his head. "Oh, heavens, no. I thought it would make an excellent souvenir of our stop. And I certainly think we've earned it. Besides, it is a rather handsome rug."

"Even if it isn't magic, Professor?"

"There's no such thing as magic, my boy." He gave me a stern look over the top of his spectacles.

"Oh, I don't know, Harmonious," Miss Bang said as she looked back at the new family being formed as Farzanah introduced her father to his new children. "I think there is still some magic left in the world."

He followed her gaze. "I think you may have a point, my dear. Perhaps there is a certain kind of magic."

AFTERWORD

As much as Scotland demands the Loch Ness Monster, Iran demands a flying carpet and a thief. And a Crackle and Bang story demands a way to make a carpet fly without using magic.

Actually, when I was trying to bring this story together, I had a huge attack of writer's block. I had a setting, but I just couldn't come up with a plot to save my life. I even reached out on a couple of online forums for suggestions. One person suggested that there was a carpet yearning to have a maiden rolled up in it. Another suggested an attack by clockwork monsters. I considered some of these ideas, but found that tearing up the market with clanks was a little too destructive for what I wanted.

I did like the idea of having a child prodigy making genius machines out of scrap, though. The rest is a question of what do you do with a thief once you catch them. Sometimes, you forgive them.

A WALK IN THE PARK

FOREWORD

The previous stories take place between *Perils* and *Kindred*. This one happens considerably later. It is actually going to be the beginning of the fourth Crackle and Bang novel, but more about that later.

Of course, the problem with hunting villains and thwarting their plots all around the world is that, eventually, one is likely to make a few enemies. And one day, those enemies are going to come hunting for you.

A WALK IN THE PARK

A s I entered New Prince Albert Park, a feeling of intense scrutiny overcame me. I searched my surroundings and noticed a woman staring at me as if I were some bizarre apparition. "You would think the woman had never seen a Cricketer before!" I remarked to my companions, indicating the oddly dressed woman with a nod of my head. The woman in question was a curious sight herself, garbed in brightly colored medieval costume and casting fearful looks in my direction from the limited protection of a canvas tent. This was one of a group of tents that appeared to have sprung up overnight just inside the entrance of the park.

"Nonsense, my boy!" declared my host, Professor Harmonious Crackle, inventor, adventurer, and man of science. "No doubt she is simply an actress who is well into her role to better represent the colonial age to her customers." He strolled ahead of me towards our eventual destination, the park's cricket pitch. I considered his words as I followed. The professor was an experienced traveler, and I supposed that he had seen such things before in his years of traveling, but there remained something about the woman's behavior that made me uneasy.

Of course, the professor was also a sight to behold, garbed with equal amounts of care and disregard. His boots were polished to a shine, but topped with a mismatched pair of spats, one white and one ivory. His baggy charcoal trousers hung off of him in contrast to his expertly tied cravat and well fitted burgundy waistcoat. His white lab coat seemed at odds with his carefully placed black silk top hat and the two pairs of goggles, one above the other, strapped about the body of the hat.

My musings on the professor's appearance were interrupted by his assistant, our other traveling companion, the lovely Miss Titania Bang, who grasped his arm and exclaimed, "Oh, an historical faire! Oh, Professor, do you think we could stop by after you've met with your informant? I do love a good historical faire!"

From my position trailing the others, I could not help but admire Miss Bang's figure. The graceful swaying of her hips accentuated by her floral skirts and the gentle play of her chestnut hair over her pale blue outing jacket as she glided into the park was almost hypnotizing. Miss Bang was the very picture of youthful innocence, her eyes bright beneath her wide brimmed hat in anticipation of a new day's adventure.

"We shall see, dear Tit," the professor replied, "You may find that you wish to stay at the game and cheer our friend on to victory, eh?" He spared her a glance and a brief smile to punctuate his point.

The past few months of traveling with Professor Crackle and Miss Bang while on my Grande Tour had shown me a great many wonderful things that I would otherwise have missed traveling by more conventional means. It had also exposed me to a number of dangers and intrigues thought to be extinct in this, the sixteenth decade of Her Eternal Majesty's reign. But some of the most memorable moments in my travels were simple pleasures, such as seeing my companions' anticipation of the cricket match.

This was the third day of the match. Several weeks ago, we had been visiting my brother in India when the professor received a message from one of his various informants indicating he had been contacted by someone claiming to have information on the latest activities of Lord Scaleslea, a traitor to the Crown and a villain of cunning and deadly intellect. While the professor traveled as a fellow of the

Imperial Society of Science and Exploration, he had been charged by none other than Her Eternal Majesty Empress Victoria herself to apprehend this fiend and bring him to suffer the justice of the Crown. The two had tangled repeatedly, yet somehow Scaleslea always managed to make his escape.

The message had called for a meeting here in Darwin, Australia during the annual Imperial Municipal League Cricket Championship. We had arrived four days prior, and discovered that local law confined *the Argos*, the professor's airship, to the port. With *the Argos* restricted to a special area inside the lightning wall that served as the city's defense, we were without our usual source of transportation. This led to us doing rather more walking than we had been accustomed to.

As fortune had it, while clearing customs, I encountered my old school chum Daniel, who had taken a posting with Imperial Customs. At our reunion, Daniel informed me that he was also a member of one of the competing Cricket teams in the championship, but that they were likely to forfeit because of a recent injury to a team member in a hunting accident. Due to a lack of available replacements, he was desperate to find a substitute in time for the championship match. He prevailed upon our friendship, and enjoined me to fill his team's vacancy and let them avoid a forfeit. Since the professor's meeting was scheduled to take place at this very match, it behooved me to acquiesce for the sake of both relationships.

The first two days had passed without event. Specifically, without the event of this mysterious informant making contact with the professor. The game itself had been fairly evenly matched and Daniel's lads were a joy to play with. We were trailing by 24 runs going into the third day, but we were all quite confident we would be able to make up the difference handily. I was more concerned that the professor's informant would fail to appear.

Thus, that morning found me walking through the park behind my companions, dressed in my second best cricket outfit with my cricket kit stuffed into a duffel slung across my back. I wished once again that I had heeded my Uncle Geoffrey's advice and hired a valet for my travels. It would have lightened my load considerably.

The tents of the historical faire appeared without herald that morning. They were white canvas affairs, each presenting a different view of life in the early decades of Australia's settlement. Actors and enthusiasts in period costumes attended each tent, presumably to expound the notable points of their particular era to visitors to the fair. At this early hour there were few visitors to the park. Most of these were pursuing a similar course to our own: a leisurely progression towards the cricket pitch.

With my thoughts come full circle, I turned and glanced back towards the woman at the first tent who had attracted my attention by with her stares. As I peered back along the path, I saw the woman in question being bodily hurled out into the pathway by someone inside the tent.

A dark clad man had shoved her out of his way with a single-armed thrust of exceptional strength. This ruffian exited the tent hefting a large apparatus whose appearance was decidedly un-historical. I found this to be most disconcerting as the device was pointed in our direction.

"Professor! Take cover!" I shouted as I dove and rolled for cover myself, hampered by the bag of cricket gear on my back. I turned my head to my companions in time to see as Miss Bang planted her hands on the professor's back and cried, "Whoopsie!" as she shoved him from the path and dropped to the ground. Then the world exploded as our assailant fired, unleashing a massive bolt of lightning at us from his gun. The bolt arced over my head, while sparks fell about me where I lay on the ground. Miss Bang lay on the pathway, unhurt, and extinguished sparks that started to ignite her crinoline. The professor pulled himself upright from the grass beside the path where he had hit the ground with some considerable force.

"I am so sorry, Professor! I tripped. You know how clumsy I can be when I am startled." Miss Bang's light tone belied any apparent awareness of actual danger in the situation.

Harmonious rose to his feet as he replied, "No harm done, Tit. But, I do believe we had best table the matter until we can deal with the present situation."

A low whine returned my attention to our attacker, whom I now realized was a woman dressed in a man's period outfit. A compressed gas canister on her back was discharging through a small turbine. As the venting gas spun the blades of the turbine, it built up an electrical charge for her weapon, allowing it to fire again with alarming speed.

I reached into the duffel I carried and grabbed the first thing that came to hand: a cricket ball. Dropping the bag, I surged to my feet and bowled at her, throwing the hard leather-covered ball overhand as if she were an undefended wicket.

The ball hurtled through the air and struck the weapon with a resounding crack, but failed to either damage the gun or knock it from her hands. She snarled at me in a most unladylike manner and trained her gun on me. As difficult to aim as a lightning gun can be, they do a most prodigious amount of damage, thus the Crown limits their use to the military. I dodged behind the bole of a nearby tree, trusting to the thick, living wood to insulate me from the blast.

Thunder filled my ears a second time as the lightnings fired from her weapon and fragments of wood exploded around me. The blast took out more than half of my shelter as the destructive power of the bolt super-heated the sap and the wood shattered from the pressure. I scrambled for a new shelter and reconsidered my strategy. I had seen military lightning rifles demonstrated at university. This one was clearly much more powerful.

"I think that will be enough of that!" declared the professor, producing his harmonic spanner from a pocket of his lab coat and fitting a large tuning fork from another pocket to the central mount. He struck the end of the fork against the palm of his left hand to activate it. Taking the spanner in both hands, he twisted the odd collection of tubes, focusing the vibrations into an invisible lance of sonic force. The mystery woman's lightning rifle screamed in her hands as Professor Crackle aimed it at her, minutely adjusting the device to tune in on a harmonic frequency that would cause the weapon to literally shake itself apart. Sparks shot from the spinning micro-turbine as the resonance in the device forced delicate parts to scrape across each other. With a high-pitched squeal and a sudden clank, the turbine seized, preventing the weapon from recharging.

Cursing vehemently, she cast the gun to the ground and shrugged out of the gas canister harness, leaving the valve open so that pressurized gas continued to hiss out through the seized turbine. This provided my first opportunity to get a good look at our attacker. She was dark haired and dark eyed, and appeared to be of Asian extraction, not surprising in this part of the world. Her hair was gathered behind her head in a loose bun. A choker with a large cameo brooch held a prominent place around her neck, having only been loosely covered by a dark cotton scarf which fell to the ground as she struggled to remove the canister. She wore a loose gray linen shirt and trews bound with a thick leather belt and calf high boots. With her hair tucked under a cap or hood and her face averted, she could easily pass as a slim Asian man. Now that she had been revealed, she stood straight and proud and the curve of her breasts could be easily discerned beneath the fabric of her blouse. Her previous behavior notwithstanding, the overall appearance was quite attractive.

She spoke, her accent a well educated European one. "Well played, Crackle. But don't think you have won yet! Your bounty will gain me access to Scaleslea's technology and I shall not surrender that lightly." She dropped the gas canister to the ground with a clatter.

"I believe you are going to find that much...", Harmonious began, but cut himself short as the strange woman turned, and ran back into the tent from whence she came. "Well, that wasn't half rude!"

I emerged from my refuge. "One cannot exactly expect manners from a would-be assassin, Professor."

He nodded, "I suppose you are right, old boy, but from the way she spoke I rather expected at least passing familiarity with proper etiquette."

Our discourse on manners was interrupted when Miss Bang inquired, "She can't possibly expect to hide in there, can she?"

The piercing whistle of a steam engine venting answered her question, accompanied by a tearing of canvas, as the tent in question was rent asunder from inside revealing a battle machine, with our still-unnamed assassin in the control seat on top. The machine unfolded to some twenty feet in height, standing aloft on two powerful, piston-like legs. The right arm ended in a massive claw tipped with sharp talons that had ripped through the canvas like tissue paper. The left sported a

Gatling gun the length of the forearm, which began to spin to life with a clatter as the machine achieved its full height.

"Oh dear. That does seem to be a problem," said the professor.

"She's mad, guvner! Run fer yer life!" came the cry from the bodiced woman whose stare had first caught my attention. She had regained her feet, but had not fled as the other members of the historical faire were currently doing. I realized then that it was not myself that she was afraid of.

Her advice seemed most apropos as the driver of the monstrosity cried out, "Die, Crackle!" and a stream of bullets erupted forth from the gun, chewing up a line of turf that narrowly missed the professor as he dodged into the woods that lined the path.

"You cannot run, Crackle! There is no place you can hide where I cannot find you! And crush you!" With that the machine pivoted and the claw slashed through the bole of the tree in front of it. The thunder of the tree's fall was punctuated by the thudding steps of the battle machine as it advanced.

The professor danced back and forth, using the cover of the trees to good effect and managing to stay half a step ahead of bullets, falling trees, and shattered tree limbs flung in his direction. His voice rose above the din, taunting his attacker with his calm tones. "I fear you overestimate your prowess, young lady. Perhaps you should give up this misadventure before someone gets hurt? Surely things cannot be so bad that this sort of behavior is your only recourse!"

The only response she gave was another volley of bullets, which ripped into the tree that the professor had just vacated.

"Harmonious!" Miss Bang cried out, her fear for him carrying on her voice. I ran over to her where she stood next to my dropped bag of cricket gear. Her eyes were bright. It was obvious that she wanted to run to him, but was only holding back due to the knowledge that there was nothing that she could do to help.

"It isn't too late for you to give this up, you know," the professor called out as he flitted into the cover provided by another tree. "No lasting harm has been done here. We can help you to escape Scaleslea's influence!"

"You stand between me and what I want, Crackle. A very unhealthy place to be." She punctuated her statement with another burst of gunfire.

We could still see the professor as he dodged from tree to tree. He appeared quite calm, despite the flying bullets and splinters as our assailant tore through the wood after him. While dodging the gunfire, he appeared to be gauging the machine for an exploitable weakness.

I turned to Miss Bang. "He's drawing her off, deeper into the wood. Go! Get help. I'll see what I can do to I can distract her and give him some time to breathe." I grabbed up my bag and fished into it for something I could use against the behemoth.

The metal body of the device appeared well armored against attack, and even provided a protective shelter for the pilot. The only reasonable angle of attack seemed to be from above, but when it was 20 feet tall and had a disconcerting tendency to knock down trees, how did one attack the relatively vulnerable top?

My hand closed upon another ball and I had an idea. This was not going to be easy. "Go quickly!" I told Miss Bang, and retrieving my spare cricket ball, I dropped the duffel again and moved off into the wood at an angle, flanking the slower but more powerful machine.

The pilot was wholly focused upon the professor and her desire to commit mayhem upon him, so she failed to note when I lobbed the ball into the air and it completely missed the mark, plopping softly down into the brush at the machine's back. I hastily recovered the ball and made a second shot, which arced down and glanced off the shell of the boiler on the back of the machine with a loud clang, but failed to garner more than a brief glance in my direction. She continued trading verbal barbs with the professor between attempts to shoot him or drop a tree upon him while sweeping it out of her way.

Her preoccupation permitted me the opportunity to move up almost directly behind her and recover my original projectile from where it had rolled after bouncing off of the lightning gun. I was extremely lucky to spy it amongst the bracken and I prayed my good fortune would not run out soon. Or perhaps this ball had been lost by some other visitor to the park. In either case, I was not about to question the provenance that placed it in my hand.

My third shot gained much more promising results. Arcing high into the air, it came down inside the cabin, missing the pilot, but bouncing off of one of the control levers and causing the device to lurch off to one side. She snarled at the distraction but quickly wrested the machine back upright. I had gathered up the previous cricket ball when I realized that the machine was no longer proceeding away from me. I looked up, only to see the spinning barrels of the gun swinging around to track onto my position.

Quite frankly, I ran, and very nearly had my legs shot out from underneath me. The burst of gunfire raked into the ground and showered my legs with splinters, dirt, and debris and the tug of it almost caused me to stumble. I was supremely lucky that she did not think I was worth more than a short burst of bullets. Had she continued firing, she would surely have riddled me with holes. I, however, was merely a nuisance to her. Having chased me off in this fashion, she pivoted, returning her attention to the professor.

Harmonious had applied this brief respite well, ceasing for the moment his attempts to dissuade her and bounding through the underbrush to a position on her flank. As he did so, he also managed to refit a different tuning fork into his harmonic spanner. He struck the fork against the tree he was using as cover and trained his device on the war machine. I was unable to discern any effect from this attack, though, as the machine turned back towards him. I heard the retort of another burst of gunfire, but the professor had already moved on to the next bit of cover.

"Things not going to plan? You know you really should reconsider this whole endeavor! Surely there are other opportunities for someone with your skills," the professor called out.

"Laugh while you can, Crackle. You can only run so long," she replied.

"And you only have so many bullets, my dear."

She responded with another burst of gunfire. While she was so preoccupied, I lobbed another shot at her. This time the ball came down on the left side of the machine, dropping into the open case that fed ammunition on a chain to the Gatling gun. It landed with a heavy chunk. If she noticed the shot, she chose to ignore it as she tried to draw a bead on Professor Crackle, who was making the most of the cover provided by the tops and trunks of the felled trees to one side of her swath of destruction. In closing with her, we had managed to pivot around her and the professor was now leading her back the way we had come.

The professor's voice rose above the gunfire. "Should I take that as a refusal, or are you still considering your options? Time is running out, you know."

"Running out for you, perhaps. I have all the time in the world!" She laughed and brought the machine forward, flipping the fallen tree tops out of her way, and eroding Harmonious' cover.

A distant crack of wood on wood sounded. I hoped that no one was stupid enough to attempt to play in the park with a pitched battle in progress!

I was now unarmed, having lost one ball inside the cockpit, and the other to the machine's ammo case. I cast about for something to use as a weapon. Spying a loose stone, I grabbed it up. It was larger than the cricket balls, but still light enough for me to throw. With another silent prayer, I lobbed it up, and was rewarded as the shot came down on top of my opponent's head with a resounding crack. The machine stopped as she clutched her head in pain. Unfortunately my lucky shot was not lucky enough to knock her unconscious.

"Quickly, man! She won't be stopped for long!" the professor called out to me. I turned and vaulted my way down the slash of toppled and decapitated trees in an attempt to catch up. The whine and hiss of hydraulics behind me indicated our mystery attacker was not yet ready to give up. Another blast of gunfire, and my left shoulder exploded in pain, turning my broken field run into a headlong tumble.

Pain shot through my shoulder again as I hit the ground. It came close to blinding my senses, but with the heat of the battle, my system filled with adrenaline, and the fight of survival, I found the strength to focus through the pain and recognize the sound of the heavy war machine closing on me. I scrambled to regain my feet, still dazed enough from the wound to neglect to seek cover as I turned to see how close my approaching death truly was.

The steam powered behemoth loomed less than six feet from me. Gasping for breath, I could only stand stunned and watch as the spinning gun raised and pointed straight at my chest. I winced, expecting to be perforated momentarily. I heard the distant sound of wood on wood again, the hiss of the steam engine, the rattle of the spinning barrels, and above it all, the click of the trigger being pulled.

Then I was sprawling on the ground again. The professor had come in from the side and tackled me, setting off another flare of pain in my shoulder.

Click-click. Click-click. We looked up into the spinning barrel of the gun, but no spray of bullets issued forth. The professor sprang into action, scrambling to his feet and helping me to mine. "Quickly, old chap! Before she realizes what happened."

Grabbing the professor's arm for assistance with my good hand, I regained my feet and we made our way to one of the park paths and hurried along it, pursued by the heavy footfalls of the sinister machine. "What happened, Professor? I could have sworn we were dead," I asked as we ran.

"I believe your cricket ball jammed the gun feed enough that the chain snapped under the strain. Effectively she ran out of ammunition before she expected to. Excellent shot, my boy!"

"I had been hoping to take out the pilot, not the gun, Professor," I admitted.

We were moving closer to the odd thock, thock sound of wood hitting wood. Our pace picked up as we left the swath of devastation and proceeded up the proper paths of the park. Hurrying along the path slightly ahead of our attacker, I look up to see the most peculiar sight of Miss Bang assaulting a tree using one of my cricket bats as if it were an axe. She spied us and paused to call out, "This way! Quickly!"

The tree that she had set upon was missing more than half of its trunk from the earlier attack with the lightning gun. Miss Bang was busily applying my best bat to the inside of that wound, using the edge of the bat as an improvised blade, with deleterious results to bat and tree alike. We half ran towards her, our main concern being to keep out of the reach of the war machine. My wound slowed my progress and the professor was unwilling to leave me behind.

Miss Bang adjusted her stance and attacked the tree at a different angle. This time her swing was answered by a crack and pop as the wood of the tree began to fail to support the weight of the upper trunk. "Yes!" she cried and applied herself with renewed vigor to further encourage the tree to fall. "Hurry!" she called.

The tree cracked and popped and began its inevitable descent. It quickly became clear that the tree was going to fall upon us. I went to step off of the path and out of the way, but the professor pulled me back, saying, "No, she has the right of it," and dragged me on in greater haste.

"You cannot lose me, Crackle! Your blood is mine," a voice called from close behind us. Thoom, thoom, thoom came the steps of the great war machine in pursuit.

The descending trunk began to rapidly gain speed above us, the sounds of its descent drowning out the heavy, rapid footfalls of the machine behind us. Directly behind us, I realized, as the professor urged me on under the rapidly descending tree. We came even with Miss Bang, ducked and stepped to one side. We turned just as the tree crashed down directly upon our assailant, felling her and her ponderous transport together. She looked up an instant before the tree struck, too late to shift the machine out of the way, and screamed, though in fear or anger I cannot say. Her cry cut off as the tree struck, dropping the machine to the ground in a grotesque parody of a man being poleaxed. It hit the ground, the weight of the tree bearing it down, and the boiler ruptured, venting steam and boiling water out over the ground.

"Are you all right, Miss Bang?" The professor's voice in the sudden quiet startled me.

"Oh, yes, Professor. Quite. Just a bit winded. How about the two of you?" she replied.

"I am no worse for wear, but I do believe our friend here has been shot."

"Oh, dear! You're hurt, my lord?" Miss Bang approached me, concern written upon her face.

"I seem to have taken a round in my left arm. Considering all the gunplay, I consider myself quite fortunate." With the excitement over for the moment, I was now able to take stock of my injuries. A few cuts and scrapes, some knocks that were sure to become bruises on the morrow. The bullet seemed to have passed through my upper arm, missing the bone, thankfully. While the wound bled on both sides of my arm, it did not appear to be serious. Now that I was no longer trying to move around and use the arm, the pain was more bearable. Nevertheless, I knew that once the adrenaline wore off I would be weak at the knees.

We were joined by the woman from the fair, who appeared holding a handful of gauzy cloth. "I'm so sorry, guvner! She just showed up one day. Took my boy, and Frank Murphy's daughter. Said if we didn't do what she said they'd be killed. Made us move the tents here this morning. We jus' didn't know what to do!" Fear and desperation were thick in her voice, tinged with regret.

As the re-enactor explained her plight, Miss Bang tore open the sleeve of my shirt with a series of short motions, her delicate hands displaying a surprising strength. She took a cloth from the woman and began using it to clean the blood away from my wound.

"Thank you, dear. Might I ask your name?" Miss Bang asked, her voice soothing.

The woman blushed as she replied, "It's Marjorie, miss." The soothing effect of Miss Bang's tone was clear as the panic drained from Marjorie's face.

Miss Bang nodded, fixing the name in her mind. She continued, "Hello, Marjorie, I am Titania. Would you happen to have any clean water?"

"I think so, miss," she said and placed the remaining cloth in my right hand before returning to the ruins of her tent. She seemed to fall quite naturally into the role of a servant dispatching her duties.

"Be careful, Professor! She may have more tricks up her sleeve!" I called out to Harmonious as he threaded his way through the branches of the downed tree towards the pinned machine.

He nodded, but continued his investigation. "I take your point, dear boy, but I do believe that the advantage is ours, at last. "

Marjorie returned, carrying a bowl filled with water. "Here you go, Miss." She didn't actually curtsy, but I had the distinct impression of one. As if the only thing preventing her from doing so was the need to keep from sloshing the bowl of water.

"Thank you, Marjorie." Miss Bang said and Marjorie practically beamed. "Please do try to hold still, my lord, or I fear I may miss something and you could get an infection," Miss Bang scolded me as I tried to twist to see the professor where he squatted, examining the wreckage pinned beneath the tree. "Professor Crackle is quite capable of handling this, you know." Her voice had returned to its customary tone, light and airy, with a child-like certainty of her facts. I sighed and desisted in my efforts to supervise his investigation. I did strain my ears a bit, trying to follow his progress by sound alone. I could hear the professor speaking in a low voice, but was unable to hear a reply, if any. A few moments later he stood and extracted himself from the branches of the fallen tree.

The professor sighed as he approached us. "I fear there is no more to be learned from this quarter. The danger is over, for now. She is dead." A look of sadness crossed my companion's faces. The loss of a life, even an enemy's life, is always a cause for mourning.

The professor sighed, and continued. "Did either of you see anything on the ground? I would swear that she threw something from the cockpit just before the tree hit." He turned and inspected the bracken for signs of the unknown object.

Miss Bang stopped him. "Harmonious, can I borrow your handkerchief? I need something more to bandage this wound."

"Certainly, my dear," he said and absently proceeded to produce a large white cloth from an inner pocket before returning to his search.

"I'm sorry, Professor, I didn't see anything. I was somewhat concerned with the state of my own skin at the time," I replied as I watched Miss Bang shake out the "handkerchief." It was closer in size to a small tablecloth.

Miss Bang folded the cloth into a large triangle, tied the two far points together and passed that loop over my head. Over her shoulder she asked, "Marjorie, could you help the professor? I believe I can finish up here." The woman nodded, putting down the bowl before proceeding to join the professor in his search for the missing object. I looked at Miss Bang as she took the last of the borrowed cloth from my hand and began winding it around my arm to pack off the wound.

"Do you think we can trust her?" I asked.

She gave me a scalding look for a moment, then her face softened as she took my point. The woman had just participated in ambushing us. She pitched her voice low to avoid being overheard. "I believe she is genuine. A victim caught up in someone else's plotting. While you went after Harmonious, she started to run off a half a dozen times, but it was clear that her own feelings of guilt compelled her to stay and try to help." Miss Bang tied one of the cloth strips tightly around my wound and nodded at the completed field dressing. "There. I believe that will hold you until we can find you a proper physician." She gently lifted my forearm and guided it into the makeshift sling she had fashioned from the professor's giant handkerchief.

"My thanks, Miss Bang."

She gave me a brief smile, "Titania, my lord. And you are quite welcome. I hope you won't take it amiss if I hope we never have to do this again."

I grinned. "Not at all."

We turned as the professor returned to us, knocking the dust from his retrieved top hat. "Are you hurt, Harmonious?" Miss Bang inquired, seeing the pained look on his face.

"Mmmmh? No. No, I am quite unharmed. But I fear I am at a bit of a loss to explain what that attack was about. A most peculiar business."

"You didn't recognize her?" I asked.

"No, although she clearly knew who we were. She was alive when I got to her, but she seemed... different somehow. Even her voice sounded different. Said that someone made her do it. She couldn't help herself. She used the word 'Possessed'."

"Did she say who put her up to it?" I asked.

"She just said 'The Cuckoo'. I have no idea whom that might be. She died before she could say more."

"Perhaps Marjorie knows something?" Miss Bang suggested.

I looked around for the woman, then carefully scanned our surroundings. "I don't suppose that either of you can see our re-enactor friend?" They looked as well, but it was clearly too late. The woman had gone.

"Do you think the entire tale about meeting an informant was just a ruse to bring you here for an assassination attempt?" I asked.

"Quite possibly, old chap, but I don't think that is of immediate concern."

"Oh? What do we need to be concerned with right this moment?" I asked.

He nodded towards the gate to the park, "The first of the constabulary has arrived and I imagine he will be quite keen to hear us explain the destroyed historical fair, the war machine, and the dead body. Not to mention the extensive damage to one of Her Eternal Majesty's parks."

"So you really were shot?"

Her Eternal Majesty's Junior Commissioner of Customs Daniel Rutherford, my old school chum, looked genuinely shocked as he gestured to the sling that cradled my left arm.

"Just a flesh wound, actually," I replied. Daniel rose as I escorted Miss Bang to the table occupied by himself and his wife Amelia. Professor Crackle was having some difficulty maneuvering past the maitre d'hotel, who seemed to think that the professor's attire was not appropriate to the dignity of the Chez Albert and attempted to block his entry. The professor raised his voice over the functionary's protests, "The police physician said that as long as our young friend doesn't develop an infection, he should be right as rain in a few weeks. He just needs to take things easy for a while. Do you mind, sir? I do have a dinner party to attend!"

Daniel hurried to Professor Crackle's rescue and re-assured the man that this was indeed a member of our party, and that no shame would come upon the establishment. Only slightly mollified, the maitre d' summoned our waiter with a wave. Miss Bang adjusted her lace shawl as she took her place at the table so that it fell more comfortably over her green velvet gown. The professor and I took our places flanking her, and I made proper introductions all around. The waiter took our orders and returned in a trice with a round of drinks.

"I am surprised he didn't check you into hospital for a few days," Daniel mused over his cocktail.

"The doctor considered it, but this wasn't exactly our first adventure, and I did have excellent immediate care. " I nodded to Miss Bang over my own drink, and she nodded demurely.

"You flatter me, my lord. One would think that you quite intend to turn my head," she teased.

"So, old sod, do you think you can manage with a few weeks of rest and relaxation while you heal?" Daniel's expression clearly said that he didn't believe that I was up to it.

Miss Bang replied before I could, "I'm sure that if he has any difficulty, Tinka will be more than willing to lend him a hand." I could feel the blush rising on my face.

"Tinka?" Daniel inquired, humor in his voice.

"A member of *the Argos'* crew. Quite capable. She's a very... handy sort." I supplied, then realizing that I was only digging myself in deeper, I changed the subject. "I do regret being the one to let the side down, Daniel. I hope the lads weren't terribly disappointed. I shudder to think what would have happened had the attack transpired at the game."

"Indeed, that would have been a disaster. " Professor Crackle supplied.

Daniel blanched at the thought. While it was just a municipal league championship, it was attended by hundreds of ministry and government officials and functionaries. Casualties among that audience could result in chaos. "Heaven fore-fend! As for the team, don't give it another thought. While the lads are disappointed about having to forfeit the championship, they are much more concerned that you were attacked in our fair city. Indeed, most of them feel like they have let you down when you so courteously stepped in to help us out."

Amelia leaned forward. "Has there been any further word about the investigation?"

"Nothing substantial, I am afraid. I spoke with the chief inspector before coming to dinner tonight," the professor explained. "He wasn't happy about revealing details of on ongoing case, but I was able to convince him that I had aided the police in similar inquiries in the past, and he agreed to share what little he had discovered. It seems the

Asian woman who attacked us in the park had disappeared from her home in Sydney some months ago."

Surprised, I asked, "They found out who she was?"

He nodded. "Yes. She had been a shop girl of some sort and had no history of violence or troublesome behavior. Absolutely nothing in her background that would indicate that she would be involved in anything of this sort. The inspector was quite vexed. It seems to be a dead end."

"But she was behind the attack, wasn't she?" Daniel asked.

"That's part of the mystery," Professor Crackle replied. "They found the other members of the historical faire, and they corroborated the statement that we were given by Marjorie, the woman who helped us in the park, and then disappeared. Two children had been kidnapped, belonging to two of the actors. Separately, of course. They were told that if they told anyone of the abduction the children would be killed, and then they would be hunted down as well. They all agreed that they had only seen the Asian woman, who identified herself to them as The Cuckoo.

"And yet when I had asked her why she had attacked us, just before she died, she said that she was forced into doing it by The Cuckoo. There appears to be another player behind the scenes here." He considered for a moment. "One that disguises his or her identity by instructing their pawns to assume the same identity."

"Was there any word on these missing children?" Amelia asked.

"Thankfully, yes." The professor sipped his drink. "They had been discovered in an abandoned warehouse. Scared and hungry, but otherwise all right."

"Harmonious," Miss Bank asked, "Did he say anything about what happened to Marjorie?" She seemed as if she dreaded the answer.

"Yes." He paused for a long moment. "I am afraid it isn't good news, my dear. I am afraid they found her body near the warehouse. A most grizzly business."

Miss Bang was visibly hurt by the news. She had apparently formed an attachment to the woman. Amelia reached across the table and covered Miss Bang's hand as a gesture of support.

Professor Crackle continued, "The police are quite up in arms over the whole affair. They hadn't had a whisper over anything going on. The are quite disturbed over the idea of someone moving military hardware of the caliber we encountered into the city without them hearing even a whisper about it.

"I suggested that it may have been assembled on the spot. It would seem that whomever this Cuckoo is, they believe that by killing me they may be able to worm their way into Lord Scaleslea's good graces. Which only shows how little they know, as he has none."

"Assembled in place? A whopping great machine like that?" I asked.

"Indeed, my friend," the professor replied. "Since we move around quite a bit with no fixed agenda, should someone want to set a trap for me, they would be best served to pick a place of their own choosing, prepare the trap, and then lure me in. In the latter, this Cuckoo has been most effective, but in the method of the trap he or she seems to have chosen for mobility. "

Miss Bang chimed in, "You are well known for your ability to improvise, Professor, perhaps they thought the best way to approach you would be to improvise as well?"

He nodded. "Quite possibly, my dear. Quite possibly."

Amelia looked worried. "Aren't you in terrible danger, Professor? If this Lord Scaleslea is sending assassins after you?"

He frowned for a moment. "While Lord Scaleslea is not above assassination, I know him well enough to know that he is not one to act through hirelings. While I have no doubt that he would not hesitate to try and kill me, he would do the deed himself. And no doubt take some time to prove his own superiority in the process. No, I don't believe I need be concerned with other assassins. But I am fairly sure that this will not be the last that we shall hear of this Cuckoo."

"You think that it is someone other than the woman at the park? And that he will return?" Daniel looked quite concerned at the thought.

"I have a feeling," he replied. "But I doubt he will return to Darwin. If The Cuckoo was established here I suspect that the police would have heard whispers of it long since. I suspect this person will move to another place to regroup and plan and hatch another plot."

"Or lay her eggs in someone else's nest." All eyes turned to Miss Bang.

"Your pardon, Miss Bang?" Daniel asked.

"Titania will do fine, Daniel," she replied. "I simply note that this person has chosen the name of a bird that is well known for leaving its eggs in other bird's nests, so that others will raise its young. I doubt that this person will establish a base of operations of their own, but will instead capitalize on whatever resources are already close at hand. Which begs the question of to whom that war machine originally belonged."

"Excellent observation, Tit!" The professor slapped the table with one hand.

"Thank you, Harmonious. You are most kind." Miss Bang seemed quite flattered.

"A chilling thought, though," said Daniel.

"Chilling, Daniel, is what the dear lady did to my best cricket bat! Using it as an axe!" I replied.

"I do apologize for that, but there was naught else available," Miss Bang insisted.

Daniel asked, "Was there nothing at any of the other tents that you could have used?"

Miss Bang sighed. "I looked. If there had been any suitable implements there, they exited the area along with the members of the historical faire."

"Perhaps in the future you should include an axe with your gear?" Amelia suggested to me.

I considered the idea for a moment. "An interesting thought, Amelia, but I am quite sure the league would say that it wouldn't be cricket."

AFTERWORD

This is actually the first Crackle and Bang story ever written. I was in the planning stage for writing Perils when Flying Island Press' Flagship Magazine announced that it was taking submissions for a Steampunk Spectacular issue. I had already planned the Crackle and Bang stories so, since I had a world and characters planned out and needed a short story, why not do a Crackle and Bang short?

This, of course, begs the question of why pick the beginning of book four? And the answer is... I didn't. At the time I was putting the story together I knew the first book was going to be in Prague, and the second one had to be in India. I also had a couple ideas for adventures in the states, so Australia was a natural stopping place along the way. "A Walk in the Park" was intended to just be a short, but after I submitted it, and it got published, I realized there was more of the story there. There really needed to be a full story about The Cuckoo, so why not just continue the story I had? And a new book was born.

Except it was book three at the time. It got bumped to book four when another idea came along: South Pacific Sky Pirates! But there will be more about that idea in another volume.

THE SHINING COG

FOREWORD

This story was originally part of Scott Roche's anthology *The Way of the Gun: A Bushido Western Anthology*. Scott came up with a world where Bushido and gunpowder came to the west together. Where trusted Martials (yes, it is meant to be spelled that way) kept the law and fair Judges passed judgment. Except, not all the Martials were trusted, and not all the Judges were fair.

And in this world, Scott included something for me: The Followers of the Clockworker. Religious adherents of a philosophical belief in a clockwork, mechanical universe. And Scott asked me to be a part of this world, and to flesh out the Followers of the Clockworker.

Naturally, I couldn't resist.

THE SHINING COG

"It has been said, that 'God does not play dice.' Many people have interpreted that in different ways. Some believe that this is an injunction against gambling in all its forms. Others feel that this is an indication that our lives are predestined, that all of our actions were set in motion by the Great Clockworker before the world was wound, and we can do none else but what we were shaped for.

"But brothers and sisters, I do not believe either of these is correct. God does not play with dice because the Clockworker would not use such an ungoverned system. Before the great wheels were set in motion, he KNEW, that eventually those wheels must go wrong. And where they have gone wrong, some hand must realign them, reset their timing, and send them into motion again.

"As Cogs in His Great Machine, this is our purpose, my people! We have been built with the power to see glimpses of the great working, and with this divine insight, we can do our best to push the Great Wheels of fate to mesh properly. This is our calling! Not to tick and turn idly along our span of serviceable lifetime, but to seek out what has gone wrong in the world and set it aright. We must repair the great work, so that the Great Wheels continue to roll towards His purpose. This is what it means to truly be a Cog!"

— MECHANIC ARMAND TINWICKET, SPEECHES
FROM THE GREAT NEVADA WIND-UP.

Mr. Fong brought the stranger another pot of tea.

The grizzled old man had ridden into town two days ago. He'd rented a room in Miss Abigail's boarding house, then sought out Mr. Fong's cafe. Other than sleep and the other usual personal maintenance activities, for the past two days the stranger had sat at a table in front of the cafe and drank pot after pot of Mr. Fong's tea. Alexander Copperspring and Horatio Hammersmith eyed the stranger from across the street in the saloon.

"Lex, I'm worried," the old carpenter said, sipping whiskey from his glass and looking through the dingy windows of the saloon.

"I know, Horatio. I'm worried, too," Alex replied. This wasn't the first stranger to come through town, but this one was different. Most of them just stayed for a night and moved on the next day. Some would spend an extra day to restock their supplies before moving on again. This stranger just sat at Mr. Fong's and drank tea. But that wasn't what really worried Alex. What bothered him most was the fact that the stranger had a pistol strapped to his leg. In Alex's experience, guns meant trouble.

Not that Alex had a lot of experience with guns. The problem was that you never knew what kind of man carried a gun. Well, you could figure out a little. The man wasn't a hunter. Hunters carried rifles, which, while just as deadly, were designed for taking down a whole different kind of quarry. No, a man who carried a pistol pretty much means to use it against one thing: men. Of course, there are some that say that carrying a pistol out on the frontier is just a wise move, as one never knows when one is going to be surprised by wild animals, or wild Indians. Some folks take the position that the Indians are just another kind of animal, but Alex never took by those notions. Wild men were men just the same, no matter how strange their customs may be. All were shaped by the Clockmaker and set in motion by his hand.

From all Alex had heard tell, a man carries a pistol, he's either in trouble, looking for trouble, or he's a Wayist.

The Wayists were the best and the worst of the lot.

A man who is in trouble, he may be jumpy, always afraid that he's been found out, but he'll generally keep his head down and try not to bring on any more trouble than he already has.

A man who is looking for trouble, he's safe enough as long as he's entertained. It is only when he's bored that he gets dangerous.

Neither of these sounded like the weather worn man who sat drinking tea at Mr. Fong's.

That meant he was a follower of the Way of the Gun, and much more dangerous. The best of the Wayists, they brought law and order to the frontier, protected the innocent, and never drew their guns while there was an alternative. There were less and less of those these days. You were much more likely to run into the corrupt sort. The ones that used their skills and their power to lord it over honest, hard working folk. Ones who took money to twist the law back upon itself until it broke clean apart. Either kind was deadly like a snake and twice as fast.

Alex looked at the man across the street and wished that he could tell which kind this man was.

Miss Elizabeth moved up to the table and swept up the empty plates in front of the two men. Hammersmith made a grab for the bottle of whiskey as if he was afraid that she would sweep it away as well. Almost as an afterthought, he poured another shot into his glass. Alex surrendered his empty beer glass to the saloon keeper's daughter, and she rewarded him with her own commentary. "You two are acting like a pair of fools. If you really must know the man's business, why don't ye go and ask him? Be a sight better use of your time than sitting here fretting like a pair of moon cows. An' if'n ye can't bring your-selves to talk to the man, maybe you could stir yourselves to do some work instead of sitting around here all day!"

"Lizabeth!" Old man O'Toole barked at his daughter. "Don't be scarin' off the customers!"

"Give it a rest, Da!" she called back to him with a flip of her long red braid. "You're not going to lose custom from me encouraging these two to go out and work up a thirst. It's not like there's another saloon in town!"

Her father grunted back at her, then went back to stocking bottles behind the bar. Elizabeth turned back to the two men who were still staring warily at the stranger across the street. "Da's not the shiniest cog in the workshop, but I expected better of you, Alex Copperspring. Most of the time you've got a good head on your shoulders. Why don't ye use it?" With that she turned and stalked off to the kitchen with the dirty dishes she had collected.

"That girl is too mouthy for her own good, 'Lex," Hammersmith said, then broke into a leer. "But awful good to look at."

"True enough, Horatio," Copperspring replied with a sigh, "but, she's also right."

"What?" The old man blinked in confusion.

"We've both got work we could be doing. The crew from Midlands and Pacific could come over the horizon any day now, finally bringing the railroad through. Our job's not done until the station is done and the rails are laid."

Horatio shook his head. "Lex, the railroad was due to come through two years ago. We're ready."

Alex grabbed his hat and stood. "We're ready for the crews to arrive, but we're not done, Horatio. You're still working on the station office, and I still need to rebuild the pump for the water tower. That's the job Midlands and Pacific gave us when they sent us out here. We'd best be about it. That man may be a gunslinger, or a Wayist, but so far, he's minding his own business. We'd best be about ours."

Setting his hat on his head, Alex dropped a coin on the table to cover his tab. "Billiards later?" he asked Hammersmith.

The older man smiled and answered, "Only if you promise not to make any of them fancy shots all around the table."

Alex laughed and headed out the doors of the saloon. He blinked in the bright sunlight as he stepped onto the porch in front of the building. Pulling the brim of his hat forward to shade his eyes, Alex shuffled forward, then stepped down into the street.

Across the street, Mr. Fong registered Alex's presence with a deep bow. Alex nodded. "Afternoon, Mr. Fong," he said with a wave. The stranger simply sat at his table and sipped his tea, not turning his head or even recognizing the other men. He didn't seem to spare any attention to any of the other folks on the street going about their business. He just sat, sipped, and waited.

Sighing, Alex turned up the street and began to walk towards the House of the Clockworker. The House marked one end of the town, the other end was marked by the Circle. In most townships, the Circle occupied a prominent position in the town square, but Bowman's Station was a town settled primarily by followers of the Clockworker. Some folk, like the Hammersmiths followed the Carpenter. Most of the farmers and ranchers that supported the town followed the Shepherd. While no one in Bowman's Station followed the Way, the law declared that each town must have a Circle for the resolution of disputes. A few of the townsfolk hard argued against building the Circle, but in the end they'd settled for moving it to the edge of the settlement rather than risk the wrath of the law. As a result, the town had taken on a barbell-like appearance with a single main road between the Circle and the House and all the main shops and businesses clustered along it. Families either lived above their shops or in separate dwellings behind them. These formed a secondary street ringing the town. Farther out, of course, were the farmhouses and the farms that provided the needs of the occupants of Bowman's Station.

Alex angled to one side of the street as he walked, aiming towards his workshop across the street from the House. He was fortunate to have such a prestigious place for his workshop. On the other side of the street, where it parted to go around the House, stood the Station and the Platform. While the rails had yet to be laid down, the site had been mapped for the station and the Yard that would one day service the railroad, and most of the buildings had been built already. Wide cleared lanes marked the path that the rails were destined to take to the station and to the rail-yard where trains could be refueled and repaired. Alex needed to stop by his shop to pick up a few tools, then head over to the Yard and get to work on the pump that filled the water tower for the trains. He was still lost in thought, cataloging the items he would need, when two more strangers nearly rode him down.

These men had come down through the path the rails were to take into town. Now they'd ridden around the station and down the main road, paying no attention to the townsfolk on the road. Alex jumped aside as the pair bore down upon him. They continued down the street at a gallop, only checking their progress when they finally came up to the Circle at the far end of the street. One of the pair, the smaller one, cursed loudly as they turned their horses around. Even from as far away as he was, Alex could hear the man yell, "What kind of back-assward town is this? Don't these dumb shits know the Circle is supposed to go in the center of town?"

Alex couldn't hear the reply from the larger man, but he could see him draw a pistol from his belt. The two of them trotted back towards the center of town, and the armed man fired two loud shots into the air, instantly gaining the attention of every person on the street.

"Listen up, people!" the larger man's voice boomed down the suddenly silent street. "Gather round!" He glared at the dumbstruck townsfolk for a moment before bellowing again. "Come on! Move it! I don't intend to scream my fool head off! Get over, here, people!" The people in the street slowly drew forward towards the two strangers, reluctant to come closer until he returned his gun to its holster. As he replaced his weapon, he opened his coat enough that a dirty metal badge could be seen pinned to his shirt front. Folks came out of their shops to gather in the street by the two men. Alex found himself drawn down the street by his own curiosity over who these strangers were, and why they had come there.

"All right, people!" the man cried again a scowl crossing this face. "I am Martial Thaddeus Black. This is Acolyte Joshua Stone." He gestured to the smaller man. At this distance Alex could clearly see the pistols strapped to each of their legs. The man drew a stiff card out of his coat, unfolded it, then proceeded to read from the card. "After a review of the pertinent documents, it is the ruling of Judge Wilcox that Midlands and Pacific Railroad did indeed fail to register a proper claim for land in this territory, and for permission to build structures upon said land. Pursuant to this ruling, Judge Wilcox has found in favor of the claim of Hanson Cumberland, and has ceded this entire valley unto his possession."

Alex could feel a fire burning in his chest. Cumberland! The cattle baron? That old bastard! *I'm sure Cumberland paid a hefty sum to get the Judge to rule that way. Old robber baron has probably been doing his level best to delay the railroad until he could lay claim to this valley. Now I bet he'll lease the right of way right back to Midlands and use the railroad to move his cattle to market after turning this whole valley into his private grazing lands."* He could feel his hands clenching into fists.

But the Martial wasn't done yet. He sneered as he continued, "By order of Judge Wilcox, all residents of this valley are hereby declared trespassers. The Judge is however willing to grant the following amnesty, those who remove themselves and whatever possessions they can carry from the valley in the next 24 hours from this reading will be granted amnesty. Any who remain after the amnesty will be shot as trespassers." He dropped the card and addressed the gathering crowd. "You got that, criminals? The Judge has given your unworthy hides a gift. Grab what you can and be over the horizon before this time tomorrow and you're free. Stay, and we start shooting." The Martial gave a cruel smirk to the crowd and laughed at their alarmed murmurs.

Alex couldn't take it any more. "That claim was legally filed and registered. I was there!" A few other townsfolk shouted agreement.

"Who said that?" Martial Black scanned the crowd, his hand reflexively returning to the butt of his pistol, and the crowd melted away in front of Alex. A rush of fear stabbed through him, but his temper was up now, and Alex fought down the fear. He'd put too much work into this place. He wasn't about to see that all swept aside by a crooked Judge.

Alex stood his ground. He looked up into the Martial's eyes and said, "I did."

Black looked into Alex's eyes for a moment, then his eyes dropped down to the Shining Cog that hung on a copper chain around Alex's neck. His hand moved from his pistol and he leaned forward on his horse and spat in the engineer's direction. "Son," he said, "It don't matter shit what you thought you saw. The Right Honorable Judge Wilcox has ruled on this, and the case is closed. You'd best high tail your ass out of town while you still have a chance. 'Cause come tomorrow, I'm gonna look forward to using a yellow belly like you for target practice." The grin that crossed the Martial's face could only be described as evil, and his acolyte started laughing high and loud like a donkey's braying.

"There ain't nothin' honorable about your precious Judge Wilcox. The man ain't never had a thought that hadn't been bought and paid for by someone else's money! He's a crook and a swindler who wouldn't know true justice if it bit him in the ass! This whole damn country is goin' straight to hell if we're to depend on the likes of a 'Judge' who sells 'Justice' to whomever has the biggest bag of gold!"

Stone sat up on his horse and yelled back at Alex, his young voice squeaking with outrage. "You can't talk that way about a Judge! His word is the law!"

"His word is available to the highest bidder!" Alex screamed back, his face going red. His pulse pounded in his ears and he felt like his head was on fire. Some part of him deep down knew he should stop, but he couldn't stop the words from tumbling out of his mouth. "And you two aren't any better. You're not lawmen. You're nothing but a couple of gun-toting thugs! If you had even a shred of honor you would have never ridden out here..." Alex never finished his tirade, because Martial Black had jumped from his horse, pistol in hand and stomped up and grabbed the front of Alex's shirt. He pulled Alex off balance and began to drag him back towards the horses.

"Boy, you have done signed your death warrant! I ain't gonna wait until tomorrow, I'm gonna have your ass in the Circle right now!" Alex grabbed at the fist twisted up in his shirt-front and tried to pull his feet underneath him.

"HOLD!" The voice boomed out with an air of authority that made everyone stop in their tracks. There was no question of doing anything but obey that voice. Even the horses stopped moving and the only sound to be heard was Alex falling to his knees.

For a second, no one moved, then there came the crunch, crunch of slow, steady steps on the sandy soil. Each head slowly turned to see the old stranger step forward from where he had sat in front of Mr. Fong's cafe.

"This is not the Way," he said. You could hear the capitalization in how he spoke. There was no doubt whatsoever that the old man meant the Way of the Gun. "There is honor in accepting a challenge, but there is no honor in gunning down an unarmed man."

Black's fist twisted against Alex's chest as he pulled on the smaller man. "Weren't you payin' attention, old man? He Challenged me!"

The stranger stepped forward again and the townsfolk slid out of his way as he moved to stand next to Black and the kneeling engineer. His tone was still even and full of authority. "I saw. I heard." He looked down at the fist wrapped up in Alex's shirt, then pointedly looked the Martial in the eyes. Black jerked his arm down, sending Coppersmith down onto the ground, and stepped back two paces.

The stranger helped Alex to his feet.

"Son, do you own a gun?" the old man asked as Alex tried to straighten his clothing.

Alex looked across at the man for a moment, then shook his head. "No."

"You ever held a gun?"

"Nope."

The stranger turned towards the two Martials. "Even the lowest acolyte is permitted time to train. This man has the right to time to acquire a gun and become familiar with its use before answering the call of the Circle." Again, you could hear the capitals as he spoke. "As an uninterested witness, I recommend he be permitted a month to train before this Challenge is decided."

"A month!?!" Black screamed, "Like hell!"

Alex turned to the old man. "What good will that do? If we're not all out of here by tomorrow, these two will shoot anyone who's left."

The grizzled man nodded. "The Judge's proclamation is bound to this challenge. It must be suspended until the issue is decided."

Now Stone piped up from atop his horse, "Who do you think you are, telling us to ignore the Judge's orders?"

He looked at each of the Martials in turn before replying. "Who I am doesn't matter. This is the Way. This is the Law. The Judge's honor has been called into question, as well as your own. This is a matter to be settled in the Circle. If you win," he gestured to Black, "the Judge's ruling will be upheld. If the boy wins," Alex bristled at being called a "boy", but the old man continued right on, "then the Judge's ruling will be overturned. This is the Law."

The stranger turned to look Alex in the eyes. His expression sober, and frowning slightly. "Unless, of course, you wish to recant your words and withdraw your Challenge."

Alex considered his situation. He'd shot his fool mouth off and was likely to get himself killed. But if he won, somehow, if he won, then the town would be safe. He wasn't sure he could bring himself to take another man's life, even with a month of training. But that would be a month more time for the rest of the town to gather their things and make a safe retreat. Alex's mouth felt dry. He swallowed. "No. I'm not going to withdraw a single word."

"That's fine by me," Black scoffed, "but there ain't no way I'm gonna give him a month to run away. He can have tonight to practice and we'll settle this at dawn tomorrow!"

"No," the stranger answered. "A few hours, even a day is not enough time. Fifteen days."

"Three days!"

"Ten."

"A week, no more!"

Alex couldn't believe that his life was being bid away like this, but before he could open his mouth to protest, the old man answered, "Agreed."

Black holstered his pistol now, and then stalked back to his horse and mounted. "The rest of you criminals can stick around to see the show. I'll even give you time to bury the fool before I start the clock." He walked his horse forward, and frowned down at Alex and the stranger. "As for you, Ranger, you better make sure he's here when we get back or I'll be lookin' for you, too. Aidin' and abettin' a felon." The Martial spat again, missing the ranger's boot by inches, then the two horsemen shook their reins and galloped down the street and out of town.

Alex looked at the stranger who'd just bought him another week to live. The old man looked back.

"Let's get to work," he said.

The door of the workshop slammed open and bounced back against the wall. Alex stalked into his workshop before the door could close and threw his dirty hat down upon the workbench.

"Dammit, old man, what the hell have you gotten me into?" Alex glowered into the darkness of the room.

"I didn't get you into anything," came the voice from the doorway. The room brightened as the weathered traveler gently pushed the door open again. "Those words were your own. I don't doubt that they're likely true enough. All I did is give you a fighting chance to back them up. I don't see you as a man who's lookin' to get hisself killed."

Instead of answering, Alex grabbed a taper and stomped over to the forge in the corner. He opened the cover and flinched as heat rolled out over him. He stirred up the banked coals with a long-handled shovel, then lit the taper. He slammed the cover down again and took the taper from lamp to lamp, lighting each and brightening the cluttered workshop.

The ranger stepped quietly into the room, calmly pushing the door closed behind him.

Alex ignored the presence of the older man, going instead to a small steam engine bolted to one side of the main workbench. He popped the hatch on the water reservoir, splashed some water in from a can on the floor, then closed and latched the hatch with a thump. He slapped closed the pressure valve on the attached steam tank and slammed open the cover on the firebox. He grabbed up a scoop of coal and stuffed it into the chamber, not caring that only about half of the fuel entered the small engine, or that the scoop bounced out and clattered on the floor when he dropped it back in the bin. Alex slammed the forge cover open again, but then ceased venting his anger as he carefully scooped up several hot coals on the shovel and carefully deposited them into the firebox of the steam engine. He closed the forge a second time and returned the shovel to its place, but he had now lost the drive to continue banging about his workshop.

The old ranger pushed his hat back on his head. "Done?"

"Not quite," Alex replied testily, "Last I heard I've got about a week left, then I'm sure I'll be done." He leaned on his workbench and scowled sourly.

"If that is your attitude, you're right. If you're sure you're gonna lose, you're as good as dead, son." He walked over to the other side of the bench, his spurs jingling as he did so. He leaned on the bench opposite of Alex and looked him in the eye. "But if you believe in yourself, and your cause, even the most unskilled man can win in the Circle." His tone drove the words home, and Alex couldn't think of a response for several seconds.

"I've never even held a gun," he said, finally, "I'm not a killer. I follow the Clockworker. We don't believe in fighting. We're pacifists. How can I kill a man in a duel?"

"You have the strength to stand up for what you believe. Despite all that you have been through, you still believe in Justice, even when the forces of the Law are turned against you. You have the Respect of your fellows, and you show more Respect than those two Martials did. You have the Courage to stand up when the odds are against you and take a stand. You have chosen your path based on the Rightness of it, and that grants you more Righteousness than those two men will ever know. You have more Honor than the two of them put together. You've got the Loyalty of the other townsfolk, and I have no doubt that you return that Loyalty as well. I've only known you a handful of minutes, but from what I can clearly see, you're well down the path of the Way. You don't need a Gun to follow the Way, you need the Way to handle a Gun." He spoke as if reciting a catechism and the capitals of each word were again clear in his speech.

He leaned back and sighed. "As for Clockworkers being pacifists, you really don't know that much about your own people, do you, son?" With that, he drew his pistol from its holster and laid it down on the table between them. Grabbing a small screwdriver from the work-bench, he pushed down on a pair of pins in the base of the grip of his revolver, pulling the pins out the other side to let them drop onto the surface of the table. With the pins removed the top cover of the grip shifted down and the ranger flipped it aside with a well practiced movement. There, underneath the cover was a steel strut that was part of the structural support for the revolver's grip, and in the middle of that strut was a small piece of polished copper. Alex recognized it as a maker's mark, the signature of the craftsman who had built the weapon. A wave of shock went through him as he looked down on his workbench and saw there, in the heart of a weapon of death, the Shining Cog of the Clockworker.

For a long minute, the only sound in the workshop was the quiet bubbling of the water in the boiler of the steam engine.

The ranger broke the silence. "Hasn't been a gun made in the last hundred and fifty years that wasn't designed and built by a follower of the Clockworker, son. A few have tried, but none of 'em have made a design worth a damn. The gun is just a tool. The measure of the man is in what you do with it. Black and his like use it to threaten, terrorize, and bully people. When that fails, he'll kill them, and wrap himself in the law so he can pretend he didn't enjoy every minute. He pays lip service to the Way, but he doesn't live it." He lifted his right hand from the table and jabbed a wrinkled index finger at the stunned craftsman. "Now, you, son, you have potential. You already know when to leave the gun in its holster. The question is, do you know when to pick it up?" He dropped his hand back to the table. "Have no doubt. Black *will* kill you if you step into the Circle and aren't prepared to defend yourself. You don't have to kill him to win, but if you're going to walk out alive, you're gonna have to shoot him, son."

Alex looked back down at the gun resting on his workbench, and the shining bit of copper that gave truth to the other man's words. He frowned momentarily at the bubbling and hissing of the steam engine at the end of the bench and let the reality of his situation sink in. He only had two chances of outliving the week: start running now, and keep running until Black or someone like him tracked him down, or face the corrupt Martial in the Circle and somehow win the duel. As distasteful as the idea of trying to harm another living being was to him, Alex didn't give himself much of a chance on the run. It wasn't the kind of life he had ever imagined for himself, and he wasn't suited for it. Just the thought of running made Alex sick. He might be scared, but he didn't want to be ruled by his fear.

He sighed. "I don't know that it makes a difference. I don't have a gun and there is no place near enough for me to get one and get back within the week." He closed his eyes momentarily, then reopened them to look into the older man's eyes. "If I'm going to be armed going into the Circle I'm going to have to build a gun."

The ranger's hands flew over the revolver, deftly disassembling the weapon into its component parts as he spoke, "I can show you how it's put together..."

"No!" Alex cried and he walked away from the bench towards the forge. He raised his voice to be heard over the racket coming from the small steam engine. "No, no, no! I can't smith those kinds of parts, they have to be cast, and I don't have what I'd need to cast something strong enough to withstand the pressure. Even if I could duplicate your revolver, it would probably explode when I tried to test fire it. I don't even know if I can make gunpowder. It's not something I ever studied."

"And if I lend you my gun, there's no guarantee they won't try something. I have to be armed to keep that acolyte honest." The ranger pursed his lips for a few seconds. "You know, your gun doesn't have to use gunpowder. It just has to be able to shoot a small projectile." He held his fingers together to illustrate the approximate size.

"Well, if I can't use gunpowder, how am I going to shoot the bullet?" Alex was practically yelling to be heard over the damn steam engine.

"I don't know." The ranger shrugged. "I thought you Clockworkers were good at solving problems." He smiled at Alex.

"WHAT? Of all the..." Alex sputtered as he felt his ire rising again.

"Now, don't blow a gasket, son."

"My name is not 'son'!" Alex screamed.

"And my name is not 'old man'!" the ranger screamed back.

Before Alex could retort, the two men were startled by a loud whooshing followed by a crack and the shrill sound of steam escaping. At the other end of the bench, Alex could see his small steam engine was now venting a narrow jet of steam at the roof of his workshop. His eyes tracked up to the roof and picked out a small patch of daylight where the locked pressure gauge of his engine had been propelled through the roof of the workshop. Dust and a few pieces of wood fluttered down to litter the floor.

Alex stepped forward and extended his hand, his eyes never leaving the hole in the roof of his workshop. "Alex Copperspring," he said.

"Diogenes Booker," the ranger replied, grasping Alex's hand.

Alex solemnly shook the older man's hand. "I think I have an idea…"

"Ye damn fool. You're going to get yourself killed, and it ain't gonna do none of us a bit of good," Elizabeth said. Her words were harsh, but the expression on her face was more of a pout. Alex looked up at her as he fumbled with the straps for his "gun". Her eyes were wet and very green, and her hair hung loosely about her face, framing that pout in a cloud of red.

The weight of the contraption dug into his waist, and he tightened the belt another notch to keep it from slipping. As he did so, he answered her, "I'm sure you're right, Miss Elizabeth. It certainly won't be the first time my big mouth got me in trouble." He grinned at a new thought. "I certainly hope it won't be the last."

Her eyes smoldered for a bit as she considered him, then her hands shot out and buried themselves in the lapels of Alex's coat. She jerked him forward and met his mouth with hers in a deep, passionate kiss. Alex's world collapsed, shutting out everything around him, until all he was aware of was the feel of her lips against his, her questing tongue, and the rapid pounding of the blood in his ears. After a wonderful eternity, they pulled away slightly and they panted to catch their breath.

His slitted eyes looked into hers and she growled breathily. "Ye better live through this, Alexander Copperspring, or I will make you regret it for the rest of yer life!" She pushed him slightly as she let go, and he swayed unsteadily on his feet as she turned with a flip of her hair and stalked back into her father's saloon. Alex blinked in the bright sunlight, and the logical part of his mind struggled to make some sense of her parting statement. He pulled at his belt absently, suddenly aware that his pants seemed to have shrunk a size or two on the spot.

Stiff leggedly, he turned and surveyed the town. In only seven days, it had become a ghost town. Most of the people had taken advantage of the time to pack themselves up and leave. The few that stayed has also packed up their belongings, but they waited to see the outcome of the duel. In the first few days after the challenge, they had treated him as a hero, toasting him and offering their help, although more often than not they simply got in his way. As the past week had drawn on, Alex's neighbors had become increasingly withdrawn, and some of them slipped off out of town in the night. Now there were only a handful left to witness today's events.

Alex walked stiffly across the street to where Booker stood with Mr. Fong. The Chinaman's cafe had been packed up into an odd little cart that was studded with little drawers containing different varieties of tea. Perched on top of the cart was a brasier that held a boiler, and a rack that held three iron pots of tea, keeping them warm and well secured when Mr. Fong moved the cart. Mr. Fong was holding one these pots, pouring tea into a small cup held by the ranger. As he finished pouring, Mr. Fong held the handle of the pot between his hands and bowed low to Alex.

"Fortune smile upon you, Mr. Alex," he said as he straightened.

"Thank you, Mr. Fong. I'll take everything I can get."

The ranger grunted a laugh and then blew on his tea and sipped it gingerly. "Keep your head, son, and you'll keep your head." He smiled at his little joke and sipped again.

Alex looked at the older man. "You really think I can survive this?"

Booker pointed his chin at Alex. "If that thing doesn't jam, and if he doesn't go for a quick head shot right off the bat, you're going to have a fighting chance. Just remember what I told you. Your biggest advantage is that he doesn't think you'll be a threat. If he tries to play with you for a bit, that gadget of yours should let you give him a surprise.

Just don't be afraid to do the needful when things get serious." He blew on his tea again and took a bigger sip.

"Yeah," Alex said. His face fell, and the trouble in his heart was plain upon it. Could he kill another man, even if his own life depended on it? Alex wasn't sure. He knew he didn't have to kill Black to win the duel, but he just couldn't imagine the arrogant Martial surrendering. He was so sure of his own superiority, he'd keep fighting to his last breath.

Booker downed the last of his tea and interrupted Alex's thoughts as he handed the cup back to Mr. Fong. "Did you light that thing up yet?"

Alex blinked, then shook his head. "No, I haven't gotten a chance. Would you mind?" He turned his back to the two men, and hefted on the two straps that snaked over his shoulders. As he did so, he could hear the water sloshing in the small steam engine on his back. It was mounted to a steel bracket that was bolted to a piece of wood that served to shield his back from the heat. He had recovered the damaged pressure gauge and managed to refit it to the engine. He'd added a new valve that would vent excess pressure and prevent the gauge from launching itself again. From the side of the pressure gauge, a thick tube stood out from the engine. It hung down, drooping almost to his knees before swinging back up and connecting to the base of the handle of Copperspring's "gun".

The gun itself stood out oddly from his leg. The handle stuck out where it could be easily grabbed, but this was mostly because of the three large tubes clustered around the barrel. Two of these were rounded cylinders linked together by steel tubing and connected to the body of the gun just above the grip. The third tube had a flat end on the business side of the weapon and tapered down to a thick tube that fed into a disk that bristled with gears. The whole apparatus clung to a magnetized metal plate strapped to Alex's leg.

Booker opened up the firebox of the small steam engine and turned to Mr. Fong. "If I could trouble you for a hot ember, Mr. Fong?" he said to the Chinaman.

Mr. Fong bowed low. "It would be my pleasure, Mr. D." With that, he pulled out a pair of long tongs and deftly picked out a hot coal from the brasier on his cart. He placed the coal in the middle of the fuel that Alex had packed the engine with earlier in the morning. As Mr. Fong withdrew the tongs, the ranger closed the hatch of the firebox and latched it down. He patted Alex on the shoulder to show they were done.

Alex turned back around. "Thank you, Mr. Fong." The small man bowed again, but Alex merely bobbed his head, unable to give a proper bow with the weight of the engine on his back.

Booker and Alex turned towards the Circle at the end of the main street. They moved slowly as the sandy soil of the street crunched underneath their boots. They passed the next few shops in silence before Booker spoke again. "You know, you really need a better way to power that thing."

Alex laughed bitterly. "Give me another month and I might be able to come up with one. It was tough enough to put this thing," he slapped the sidearm, "together in a few days. I've hardly had any time to practice with it. I'm still not sure if I can hit what I'm aiming at."

"You'll do all right. You're better than some acolytes I've seen."

"I'm not up against a acolyte."

"No, no you're not." They walked on in silence for a few seconds. "You're up against a gunslinger and a bully. He's been given the title of Martial, but he doesn't deserve it." He reached out and stopped Alex. The two men stood and Booker looked Alex in the eyes. "He might have been worthy of the name, once, but he's not now. Don't build him up into an unstoppable opponent. He's not. He's lost the Way. He's just a man." The ranger put one finger against Alex's chest. "You have the Way, even if you don't believe it. Don't worry about living or dying. Don't worry about killing. Just do what is right, and trust in God to see you through."

"I don't think this is what the Clockworker had in mind."

"The Clockworker, the Shepard, Justice. Those are just labels, son. Symbols to help us come to grips with a power we can't begin to understand. God sets us on the paths we need to walk down. Trust in him to guide your steps, even when it seems like he's changing your path."

Alex stared into the older man's eyes for several seconds. "I never would have pegged you as a religious man." He could feel a smile creeping over his face. A similar one appeared on the ranger's face.

"No one ever does," he said and started down the street again. Alex hurried his steps to catch up, and he could hear the water behind him beginning to bubble in the steam engine.

The Circle of Bowman's Station was a large metal ring pounded into the ground at the end of the main street. Inside the ring, concentric circles of paving stones filled in the Circle, with a single large stone in the center. Six feet out from the ring were a series of iron wood panels planted deep into the turf, each forming a barrier that appeared to be six feet square. Another six feet out were another series of identical panels that filled the gaps between the first set. The panels had been set to protect the surrounding buildings from stray shots in a duel, but they'd never been used. Until now.

As Alex strode between the thick wood slabs, it struck him for the first time that the panels set around the Circle turned the whole thing into a large gear. One more piece of defiance from the citizens of Bowman's Station. The thought helped put a spring back in his step.

Looking around, Alex couldn't see another soul. No one had come to give their support, or even witness the event. His spirits sank for a while until he looked up at one of the few buildings that faced the Circle. Over the array of panels, he saw the windows of the second floor of the building, and behind those windows, the waiting faces of a few of the town's remaining residents. Someone noticed him looking, and waved, but through the glass Alex couldn't tell who. He waved back and glanced over to the building on the other side of the street. A few faces peered out from there, too. His people hadn't abandoned him, they just wanted to watch at a safe distance. *I don't blame them,* Alex thought, *I'd rather be up there watching than down here.*

Alex wandered over and leaned against one of the panels to wait.

The steam engine on Alex's back was chugging away merrily by the time horses could be heard approaching. Alex started to cross to the other side to watch, but Booker put his arm across his chest to stop him. "Not yet," he said, but didn't offer any more. Alex looked down and realized he'd been about to cross into the Circle. Apparently there were rules about such things that he hadn't learned yet.

They stood and heard the sound of two horses pulling up outside the Circle. Over the sound of the engine, Alex could barely hear Black and his apprentice talking. "What the hell is with these things?" asked the acolyte.

"I dunno. Maybe they can't shoot straight. Too afraid of gettin' a hole or two in their precious houses." Black snickered and Alex could hear his boots crunch to the ground as he dismounted. "Let's go see if the coward showed up."

"What is that sound?" Stone asked, but the Martial didn't bother to answer.

Alex followed the sound of boots until the two Martials hove into view between two of the flats surrounding the Circle. As soon as he saw Alex, the Martial let out a whoop. "Well lookie here! Looks like tinker-boy's got some guts. You ready to die, little man?" He laughed evilly. Stone giggled, a high, squeaky sound.

Alex did his best to keep his face calm. His voice was even as he answered, "Are you?"

"OH! Oh, I am SO scared!" Black teased and laughed. "And what the hell is that thing strapped to you? You gonna fly away with that thing?"

Now Alex smiled. "I didn't have a gun, so I had to make one. Wanna see if it works?"

The acolyte let out another squeaky giggle, but Black seemed to sober. "Buzzards gonna be picking over your bones, soon, boy." He grabbed the edge of his coat and pushed it behind him, using his left hand to hold the coat behind his back. "Let's do this!"

As if on cue, Booker and Stone both moved several paces to their right around the Circle. They faced each other at ninety degrees from

Alex and Black, and several paces back from the metal band that defined the edge of the Circle.

Booker spoke first, his words practiced, as if he was reciting a litany. "A challenge has been issued and accepted. You stand on the brink of judgment. This is your last chance to turn back."

Stone turned to Alex and picked up the recitation, "Challenger, do you wish to recant your challenge?" The boy's voice broke slightly at the end.

Alex remembered the words that the ranger had taught him the night before. "I will not recant. The challenge stands."

The old man turned to face Black. "Defender, do you wish to yield to the challenge?"

The Martial spat. "I. Will. Not. Yield." His voice was low and dangerous.

The witnesses turned to face each other. Alex realized that their places were chosen to put them out of the line of fire and let them see the duel happen. Booker's voice rang out again, "Enter the Circle."

Alex matched Black step for step as the two of them walked into the Circle, stepping up onto the cobbles. Black held his right hand out from his body. Alex kept both hands out from his body, his coat already being held out of the way by the straps that bound the steam engine to him.

The witnesses responded in unison, Booker's voice carrying over Stone's. "The Circle has been entered. Only the Victor may leave." The two of them bent into a crouch so that they could move quickly in either direction. Alex watched the Martial's hand and leaned his weight forward onto his toes. For a minute, the two of them stood motionless, each waiting for the other to react first. Alex could feel a trickle of sweat running down his face and he wished that he could wipe it off.

Black bounced on his toes, letting out a small whoop, but Alex didn't react, watching as the gunslinger's hand moved away from his body as he dipped down. He bounced again, still not making a move for his weapon. Alex tensed and prepared to move.

The third time the Martial bounced on his toes, Alex saw Black's right hand flash towards his body, and Alex pivoted to his left, raising his arms to protect his head as he ducked and spun. Black's pistol boomed behind him, and Alex felt more than heard the Pang! as the bullet slammed into the steam engine on his back. He staggered, but checked himself before he stepped outside the Circle. He turned back to face the Martial. His ears rang, but the steam engine still seemed to be running.

"Oh! Oh, ho! That is not fair!" cried the Martial. "That thing is like armor. You just gonna keep turning your back on me, yellow man?"

Booker answered calmly. "There is no prohibition against armor. It is rarely used, however."

"Is that so?" Black replied without taking his eyes off of Alex. Alex watched the other man's right hand, now weighed down with his pistol. He gestured with the hand, never quite bringing it into line. Alex silently cursed himself for not taking the opportunity to grab his own weapon. The two men began circling each other, moving to the left. Out of the corner of his eye, Alex could see the witnesses moving to keep pace.

Alex spun back to the right, remembering this time to grab for the grip of his "gun". He was almost knocked over as he did so, Black squeezing off two rounds into his back as he turned. Alex felt like he'd been kicked and he felt the burn as scalding water spilled down his back. His scream was drowned out by the keening whistle of steam escaping under pressure. He kept his grip on his weapon and reached across his body, squeezing the trigger and causing the disk to rotate one position. With a quiet "fup" sound, the barrel released a burst of compressed air and shot a ball bearing across the Circle. Alex had hardly aimed, so it was no surprise that he missed Black and his bullet smacked into the heavy shield panels with a loud crack and bounced back at him. Alex hopped and danced to the dying whistle of the engine strapped to his back as he tried to avoid his own bullet and turn himself to face Black again.

"Awwwww…" the Martial mocked Alex, "Looks like it that thing really did work. Too bad it's broken now! So sad!" A sneer crossed the other man's face as he lifted his pistol again.

Alex pulled his trigger again and held it, the geared disk spinning, and the barrel emitting a rapid "fup, fup, fup" as it sprayed a line of ball bearings out, the twin pressure chambers attached to the gun provided the force behind the small projectiles. The line of his fire intersected Black's legs and blood blossomed across his trousers as the steel projectiles tore through the muscles of the Martial's legs. Black fell to the ground screaming.

"Oh, Shit!" Stone gasped and scrambled for his own gun, getting tangled in his jacket as he did so.

"Leave that right where it is, son," Booker said quietly, but his voice carried clearly through the air, and his tone demanded obedience. His pistol was in his hand and was aimed directly at the acolyte's head. "No one has violated the code of the duel yet, don't you go startin' now."

Stone wordlessly moved his hands away from the his gun and took an additional step back from the Circle. Booker continued to stare him down for a moment, then returned his gun to its holster. Alex waited, but neither man moved again, and the only sound was the moaning and sobbing as Black grabbed at his wounds and rocked back and forth on his side. Alex let the barrel of his gun drop and took a step towards the downed Martial.

With a sudden, animal scream, Black grabbed his gun from the stones of the Circle and rolled over to face the engineer. The man's gun boomed again and Alex's leg flared with pain that blinded him, turning his world into a red haze. Alex swayed, off-balance, and then his leg gave a sickening crack and a fresh spike of pain shot through him as he fell. The air rushed from his lungs as his body slammed into the ground and the rough stones bit at his hands and face. Alex's gun rattled as it bounced off the stones and tried to skitter away from him but was checked by the tube connecting the gun to the ruined engine strapped to Alex's back. Alex wanted to cry out and give voice to his pain, but all that came out of his mouth was a weak, mewling whimper.

A low, grating laugh carried across the Circle. Alex pushed himself up onto his side and saw Black slowly dragging himself back to his feet. The motion sent fire running up his right leg. He looked down to see his leg bent at an odd angle, an extra bend at the bloody mass of fabric right above his knee. The laughter got stronger and louder as the

Martial pulled his injured legs underneath him and stubbornly forced them to bear his weight. He grunted as he heaved himself back up and stood on his feet again.

Alex's eyes dropped from the other man's grinning face to the pistol in his hand, and his survival instinct engaged itself once again. Ignoring the further protests of his ruined leg, he flailed with his right hand, trying to grab his gun again. His hand swiped short of the gun once, then twice, before he realized he could use the pressure tube to pull it to him. He grabbed at the tube and the gun rattled as it bounced a little closer to him. Again he grabbed for the gun, this time his palm slapping the grip and his fingers curling around it again before his wrist screamed with pain. Black had closed the distance between them and now stood looking down at Copperspring, his boot grinding Alex's wrist into the stones of the Circle. His arm stretched out in front of him and pinned to the ground, Alex looked up at his opponent.

The Martial's dark hair stuck out from his head at odd angles and dirt and blood was stuck to the side of this face. Triumph was written large upon his face as he smirked down at the tinkerer. "You... you think you can beat me, boy? Your kind can't even begin to come close!" He spat and the huge glob of spittle shocked Alex out of his paralysis when it splattered across his face. He blinked and shook his head to clear his eyes. Above him Black continued to gloat. "You don't have the will! You don't have the guts!" The Martial brandished his pistol as Alex looked desperately around him for something he could use. Some advantage. He was propped up on his ruined steam engine, his left hand was free, but he already knew he couldn't reach the gun with his free hand. He stared down his arm at the useless weapon. It should still have enough pressure stored in the tanks for a few more shots, but now it was pointed at one of the shield panels. Alex couldn't bend his wrist enough to point the barrel at the screaming man above him, even without the Martial's boot grinding his hand into the cobbles.

"You're weak!" Black screamed. "You people are nothing but a bunch of sheep! You should follow the Shepherd instead of the Clockworker! You think you fix things, but you're all broken! BROKEN!" Alex could feel his cheeks begin to heat as the Martial's words sparked his ire. *Broken? We're not followers! We're out here on the frontier! We do our part and we find a way… find a way.* Alex's anger drained away and his thoughts went into high gear, dozens of scenarios running through his mind as he considered all the angles.

"You stupid little *Cog*," Black made the word into an epithet and put all his venom behind it. "You're broken, and that's how you're going to die. A shattered little piece of metal good for nothing but scrap. And I'm the one who's gonna send you to the scrap heap."

Alex strained to lever his wrist up, his anger back and giving him the strength to fight through the pain. He angled the gun up a few degrees, adjusted it just so. *There.* Holding his hand in place, Alex looked up at Black.

"Time to die, you piece of shit," the Martial said and pointed his pistol at Alex's head.

"No!" Alex snapped. "I'm not broken. You are. And I'm going to fix you." Black's lip pulled back, exposing his teeth, and Alex squeezed his trigger and held it for a moment. The disk spun and a quiet fup, fup, fup sounded through the stillness of the morning, followed almost immediately by a crack, crack, crack! A split second later the right side of Black's head exploded in a spray of blood and meat as the steel bearings from Alex's gun punched through bone and brain and exited the Martial's body.

Alex stared as blood dripped from the ruin of Black's ear onto his shoulder. His vacant eyes remained fixed on Alex's for a moment longer, then he began to list to one side and toppled like a falling tree. The corpse hit the ground like a sack of wet suet. Alex released his gun, which clattered on the stone. He flexed his wrist, the pain lessening now that Black's boot was no longer pinning it to the ground.

"Bank shots," Alex murmured. "I always liked bank shots." Then his eyes rolled back into his head and he surrendered to the arms of oblivion.

I t was dark.
     No, there was more to it than that. It was dark, but there was something else. Something else. What was it?

Alex drifted along for a moment, trying to identify what it was that had caught his attention, not yet aware enough to marvel at the fact that he still had enough of a self to be aware that something had changed.

Oh, yeah, he thought, as he realized what it was: there was no longer a hard lump jammed up against his back. In fact, he seemed to be lying flat. It was nice, not like he was lying on the ground bleeding his life out, which he was sure he must have already done. Death was soft. It was comforting somehow. He reveled in that sense of comfort.

Wait, there was something else. Like the memory of something. Something he had heard before.

It came again. A sniffle? *Can the dead hear?*

Alex responded on instinct and made a number of discoveries in quick succession. First, he discovered that it was dark because his eyes were closed. Second, he discovered he still had eyes. He also discovered that there was a lot of light outside of his eyes, because when he opened them, it flooded in and caused new pain to lance through his head, convincing him to close them again. A low moan escaped from somewhere near him. His last discovery was that there was still other pain, but it was at a distance somehow. If he looked for it, it was there, but it was very easy to just ignore it, so he did.

After a while, he decided to try opening his eyes again, but slowly this time. When his eyes didn't complain about a little bit of light, he let in some more. The light began to resolve into an image, but it took him a while longer to make sense of it. Finally he realized that he was looking at an expanse of plaster. The light, which was still rather bright, came from somewhere to his right, and odd shadows seemed to play across the expanse. He looked curiously at it for a few seconds before it occurred to him that he was looking at a ceiling. A ceiling meant he was in a room, and there might be other things in the room.

He brought his eyes down and glanced about him. He was indeed in a room. It appeared to be his room, a small upstairs room he rented in Mrs. Reed's hotel. There weren't many visitors through Bowman's station yet, so she was happy for the trade. It also meant that Alex didn't have to worry about housekeeping or maintaining a living space attached to his workshop.

Alex wondered for a moment who would take over the workshop now that he was dead. He considered this lazily for a bit until a more rational portion of his brain pointed out that if he was dead, he shouldn't be able to feel pain. Alex checked again, and the pain was still there. *I guess I'm alive after all.*

The sniffle came again.

Since he appeared to be alive, and at least had eyes, Alex decided to take a look at what was making the noise. He rolled his eyes in that direction, and something appeared at the edge of his vision. He couldn't quite make out what it was, so he tried to move his eyes further and everything shifted as his head turned in response to the request. Another low moan sounded through the room.

The shape resolved itself into a person. A long fall of red hair hung down over the person's face and bosom, for it was a woman, and a delicate hand disappeared into the curtain of hair holding on to a handkerchief. Alex tried to speak, but his throat was dry and he croaked hoarsely instead.

The head came up quickly and the curtain of hair fell away, revealing Miss Elizabeth's face. She raked the hand with the handker-chief across her face, clearing the straggler hairs that tried to remain in front of it. Her eyes were red and puffy, and he could see the trails that tears had left as they had fallen down her face. Her nose was red and irritated from the constant rubbing with the handkerchief. She looked horrible, but at that moment she was the most beautiful thing he had ever seen.

Her eyes had flashed with a moment of panic when she first looked up at him, but that faded away as he smiled at her and a wry smile of her own began to form. Alex swallowed and tried to talk again. "Hi," he managed to whisper.

In answer, she leaned over him and kissed him. He squealed into her lips and she withdrew, looking scared. "Oh my God, did I hurt ye?"

"My hand," Alex whispered, and the two of them looked down at his right hand, his wrist wrapped in a thick bandage, and his fingers caught in the grip of her hand, with her nails digging into his palm. Elizabeth hastily released his hand and the pain subsided.

"Oh, I'm sorry, I'm sorry, I'm sorry," she babbled as she picked up his hand gently in both of her own. She knelt next to the bed where Alex had been placed and began kissing his fingers repeatedly with an additional "I'm sorry!" between each kiss. After she had addressed each injured digit and each of the nail marks on his palm she held the hand up against her face, fresh tears running down her cheeks. She was crying again, but now these were happy tears.

"It's okay," Alex answered, slurring slightly, but beginning to gain better control of his voice.

"Well," she said, regaining some of her usual tone and demeanor. "Would ye mind if I tried again, then? Ye know I don't like leaving a job half done."

"I don't think so."

She placed his hand gently down on the bed and stood up again. Then, carefully placing her hands beside him on the bed, she slowly leaned over and very thoroughly and deliberately kissed him.

As she withdrew again to her seat after an indeterminate amount of time, Alex inhaled deeply, savoring the scent of her that lingered above him. He sighed.

"Was that better?" she asked.

"Oh, I must confess I quite liked that."

She smiled. "Behave yerself, boyo, and ye just might get another," she teased.

Alex looked around the room briefly, taking stock of the situation. His hat was sitting on top of the chest of drawers, but there was no sign of any of the other clothes he had been wearing. He noticed that someone had put him into a nightshirt before tucking him in bed. Everything seemed clean and tidy, but something felt... odd. His gaze returned to Miss Elizabeth. "So, what happened?"

She was holding his hand again, and she squeezed it gently. "Ye won, Alex! Ye beat him!"

Alex got a momentary flash of the dead man standing over him. His vacant eyes still locked with his as the blood oozed from the hole in the side of his head. Alex's stomach lurched at the memory. He swallowed, and got his stomach under control before continuing. "I know. I meant, what happened after?"

"When neither of ye moved, the ranger and the boy what came with Black went to see if either of ye had survived. The Martial was dead, of course, but when they found ye were alive, the boy came running, pounding on doors and yelling for a doctor."

"Stone? Black's acolyte did that?"

"Sure'n he did! The old man stayed with ye to try to stop the bleeding. You'd lost a lot of blood, love."

"Why did he do that?"

Elizabeth shrugged. "I dunno. Part of their code or something, I guess. Ye lived through the fight, so I guess to him that was God's way of saying you were right. What boy that age is going to go against the will of God? So he went to find ye help."

Alex's brow furrowed. "Who did he find? We don't have a doctor, and the farrier was one of the first to leave."

She grinned impishly. "Mr. Fong, of all people! Apparently he was some kind of healer back in China. When he got here, no one would go to a Chinaman doctor, except other Chinamen, and they were all with the railroad. The railroad wouldn't hire him as a healer, so he became a cook. It let him gather the herbs he needed or some such thing. From there he just kept feeding folk one way or another."

"He sewed me up?"

She bit her lower lip. *Ut oh,* thought Alex, *That's not good.* She looked about the room as if trying to find something to help her avoid answering his question. "Not exactly," she said, keeping her gaze diverted.

"What do you mean?" Alex pushed his hands against the bed, trying to shift himself up into a sitting position.

"No! Don't!" she cried and put her hands on his chest. "You're not strong enough yet. Please, please! Just lie back and rest."

Alex breathed in her scent again. He wanted to do just that, rest, but he knew he couldn't get any rest until he found out how bad it was.

"Tell me."

Elizabeth sighed and moved to sit on the edge of the bed. Her hands fluttered over his chest, straightening the front of his nightshirt and pointlessly smoothing his blankets. Alex enjoyed the feeling of being touched, but he refused to let that distract him. Elizabeth wouldn't look him in the eye. "The Martial... He... He shot ye in the leg, Alex." Her voice had become very small. She swallowed. "The... the bullet," she paused for a long moment. "The bullet shattered the bone. It snapped." She tried to stifle a sob, and almost succeeded. "Mr. Fong tried, he really tried, but if he kept trying to save the leg, he was afraid he would lose ye." Her chin wrinkled up in that way that meant that she was about to start crying again. "They had to take the leg. Ye lost a lot of blood. We weren't sure ye were going to make it. I.." Now her eyes flicked to his and the tears began again. She brushed a hand against his cheek. "I thought I was going to lose you."

"I'm still here."

Someone cleared their throat, and Elizabeth stood up quickly and wiped away her tears with her handkerchief before turning to face the figure at the door. Alex looked up and saw Booker standing in the doorway, a knowing look on his face.

"How's our patient?" the old man asked.

"Among the living?" Alex suggested. "Mostly."

He nodded. "That's good enough." The ranger turned to Miss Elizabeth. "He take any fluids yet?"

She shook her head, then turned back to Alex. "Would you like something to drink, love? Are ye thirsty?"

Alex licked his lips. "I could do with some water."

She grabbed up a glass from the table beside the bed. A long metal tube was sticking out of the top of the glass. The tube was curved so that it was more of an arc. She held the glass in front of him so that the end of tube was right in front of his lips. He sucked the water through the tube, slowly at first, but then greedily as he began to realize just how thirsty he was. Soon came the stuttering, sucking sound that indicated that the glass was empty. Elizabeth straightened and said, "I'll just go get ye some more." Taking the glass with her, she moved nimbly around the bed, past Booker and out the door.

"We weren't sure you were going to make it, son," Booker said as he stepped up to the foot of the bed. "I'm glad you did."

Alex nodded. "What happened with Stone? Liz tells me he's the one who went looking for a doctor for me."

Booker nodded. "Yup. Joshua's not a bad kid, really. He just fell in with some folks who were a bad influence. He'll be all right."

"So he's still here?"

Booker gave his head a single, quick shake. "Nope. I sent him back east. Told him to go to Midlands and Pacific and tell them what happened here. Then, of course, he had to go report to the Judge. He should be back any day now."

"He's coming back?"

"Boy's gotta finish his training, better that he do it with me."

"What about the Judge?"

"If he sticks to the letter of the law, there's nothing he can do. You won your appeal fair and square. He may not like it, but he'll have to find a way to live with it. Besides, if Midlands reacts the way I expect them to, they'll be sendin' their own men to make sure the rails come through here right quick."

"They've been draggin' their feet this long, what makes you think they'll hurry now?"

Diogenes Booker smiled. "Cumberland was payin' 'em off until he could grab their claim on the valley. They put up with it because he promised that he'd honor their right of way and let the railroad go through. Now you've made it possible for them to keep the title to the valley and the bribe Cumberland gave 'em. And now that Cumberland wants it, the value of the land has gone way up. They'll make a pretty penny of of it."

"Ah," Alex said, or tried to. About halfway through, it turned into a big yawn. "Excuse me."

"No problem, Alex. Rest easy. Take the time to heal."

"I don't know, Booker. Sounds like I've got a lot of work to do. I need to get back on my feet pretty soon."

"Foot," the ranger corrected.

"Feet," Alex countered. "I'm a Cog, remember." Pride came through in his voice as he said the word. "We see a problem, we fix it." He yawned again.

Booker waved at him. "We'll argue about it later, go ahead and rest," he said, but Alex was already asleep.

"I wish ye dinna have to go," Elisabeth said as she sprawled on the bed.

"So do I," Alex replied while he sat on the edge of the bed and buttoned up his shirt. "But I'll be back soon enough. Booker says it is really just a formality. You can't officially become a Martial until you've done a circuit of the territory."

She leaned her head on her hand, and traced her other hand lightly down Alex's back. "I still can't believe that yer doing this."

Alex snorted. "You and me both. It just… just seemed like the best thing to do to protect the town."

"Some folks think ye've betrayed yer faith."

He twisted to look at her. "They're wrong. I don't expect them to know that, but I want to know that you do. I haven't turned my back on the Clockworker, I've just… I've found another way to repair things that have gone wrong. I have to do this."

She scooted closer to him. "I know. My people have always followed the Carpenter. We build. And we forgive those who seek forgiveness."

"Do I need forgiveness?"

"Perhaps. But not from me. Sometimes I wonder if ye need to forgive yerself."

He leaned down and kissed her briefly. Alex reached to the night-stand and picked up a large brass winding key. He reached down and found the hole in the side of his pants leg, and feeling with his finger, he aligned that hole with the one cut in his boot. Pushing a sliding cover aside he fitted the key into his right leg and began winding.

"There has got to be a better way of doing that," Elizabeth remarked.

"I've come up with a couple, but I haven't had time to build them. When I get back I'll see about setting up a power winder. That will make things easier in the mornings. This is much more practical for the trail, even if it does take a while."

Elizabeth sighed, then got up and began getting dressed as Alex continued to wind. She had just finished when Alex was done, and she waited while he stood and finished putting on his pants, then added his gun belt on over it. The odd weapon still looked like a cluster of four tubes, but the latest incarnation was much sleeker and more compact. On his left hip, Alex now carried a traditional gunpowder bullet pistol. He wasn't as happy with it, but he had to admit that it was more practical for the trail than having to re-charge the pressure tanks of his pneumatic gun. He still preferred his homemade weapon. Much quieter and a better rate of fire.

Elizabeth handed Alex his coat and she followed him as he shrugged into it while stepping into the hallway. The two walked in companionable silence down the stairs at the end of the hall and out the door of the Saloon, the only sound being their footsteps and the gentle ticking of Alex's leg. O'Toole glowered his disapproval from behind the bar as they passed through, but it had been months since he had dared to utter a word about his daughter's choices.

They stepped out onto the street to the sound of hammers and saws. Alex looked towards the Circle to see the forms of two new buildings looming up on the far side of the Circle. Diogenes Booker stepped away from the pair of horses and the pack mule that he had been tending.

"Morning, Alex. Morning Mrs. Copperspring," he said.

"Not quite yet, Mr. Booker, but ye bring him back and we'll take care of that right soon." She took Alex's left arm possessively and flashed a catty grin.

"I've no doubt you will, ma'am," Booker answered. He shifted his attention to Alex. "New leg?"

Alex blinked. "Yes. How could you tell?"

"It's quieter. And you seem to be moving a little better." He gestured to Alex's custom sidearm. "Did you pack a steam engine for that thing? Gonna make an awful racket on the trail."

Alex slapped his right leg. "Pressure pump built into the leg, but I have to walk around a bit to charge it. I also came up with a small engine I can stick into a campfire. If all else fails, I've still got your present."

Booker grunted. "I shoulda known."

The sound of someone running drew closer and they looked up to see Joshua Stone running down the street, a pack and saddlebags bouncing on his back as he dodged among the horse and foot traffic that now swelled the streets of Bowman's Station. The past year had made big changes in both the boy and the town. Joshua was a young man now, as earnest and forthright as he had been cruel and bullying the year before. Diogenes had been right, the boy had just needed a good role model. The town had gone from a sleepy village in the wilderness to a boom town, swarming with traders and railroad men. The track crew hadn't made it quite this far, but Alex was sure that they'd move through Bowman's station before he completed his circuit. He hoped he'd be here when the first train service started. A lot of money was moving through the town now. Quite a lot of it belonging to Hanson Cumberland, who was now paying to lease a large part of the valley from Midlands and Pacific.

Joshua pounded up to stop in front of them. Panting, he greeted them, "Ma'am! Ranger. Sir."

"No need to call me, sir, Joshua. You're the one who's the full Martial, now. I'm still in training," Alex quipped.

"I know, sir, but, beggin' your pardon, I don't think I'll ever be more than a Martial. You're meant for greater things, sir. You'll be a Judge soon, I just know it."

"Yes!" hissed Elizabeth, tightening her grip on Alex's arm.

"Let's not get ahead of ourselves," Alex said. "Plenty of work to do before that happens." Alex noted that Booker didn't say anything one way or the other.

"Yes, sir!" Joshua answered.

"Joshua! Are you going to quit 'sir'ing me, or am I going to have to start, 'Martial'ing you?" Alex's tone was firm, but he couldn't keep a smile from spreading across his face.

"No, sir, um, I mean, yes, um, Alex?" the young man sputtered to an uncertain stop.

"That's better."

"I fetched your saddlebags and your trail pack, um, Alex. I got the right ones, didn't I?" He pulled his arms forward to display the pack and saddlebags that Alex had packed the night before. "They were the only ones I saw in the workshop."

Alex nodded. "You didn't have to do that, Joshua, but thank you, just the same."

"My pleasure," he said and went to secure the luggage to one of the waiting horses.

Booker watched him go. "He's shaped up really well."

"You think he'll be all right while we're gone?"

"I do. You've been a big influence on him, Alex."

"Me? You're the one who trained him."

"I know, but he's looked up to you. You're the example he wants to live up to."

Alex didn't know what to say to that, so he said nothing.

"You ready to go?" Booker said after a moment.

"If we can get breakfast before we head out…" Alex began.

Booker grinned. "No need. Mr. Fong has taken care of that. Packed us breakfast and lunch to eat on the trail. We'll have to cook our own supper."

"Oh," Alex said. He thought he'd planned this trip out, but it didn't occur to him until now to ask if Booker could cook. He began to wonder just how well they would be eating on the trail.

"Saddle up. The sooner we get started, the sooner we'll be done." Booker moved off to his horse and mounted.

Alex turned to Elizabeth. "I guess this is goodbye, for now."

"Hurry back."

"I will."

They shared a long, tender kiss, then parted. "Be safe," she told him.

"I will."

Alex strode over to his horse, the horse that had belonged to Thaddeus Black and placed his left foot carefully in the stirrup. *I hope this works*, he thought, imagining how difficult the next month or so would be if he couldn't manage to get himself onto his horse. He gripped the horn of the saddle and bounced on his artificial leg, once, twice, and then lunged upwards pushing off with his left leg and lifting with his stump to make sure the heavy clockwork appendage would clear the horse's rump. He swung the leg over with room to spare and sat heavily in the saddle. The horse shied a little at the sudden weight, but then settled down quickly. Alex reached down and adjusted the clockwork leg until his mechanical foot tucked neatly into the stirrup. He looked over to Booker, who nodded, then turned his horse towards the Circle, the pack mule trailing behind. Alex gave Elizabeth a final wave and turned after the ranger.

"It's going to be a damned fine courthouse," Booker said as they rode.

"I guess. I just can't believe you're doing this," Alex answered, waving at the other building under construction across the street from the courthouse.

"I'm an old man, Alex. I've been riding around for over thirty years finding men and training them. A few women, too. It's about time I stood in one place and let them come to me."

"What did you think about what Joshua said? About them making me a Judge?"

Booker gave the younger man a slow look, then turned back to the road ahead of them as they skirted around the Circle. "If'n you don't fight it, I could see it happen. That's really up to you."

Alex considered these words as they rode between the two construction sites and down the road out of Bowman's station.

Booker interrupted his reverie. "Got somethin' for you." He dug into his vest pocket and pulled an object out. "It's a little bit early to give it to you, but I figure you'll be wanting it soon enough." He reached over and put the item into Alex' hand.

Alex looked down at the object in his hand. It was made of silver, a Martial's badge. But around the outside someone had added an additional band of copper marked with square notches to form a gear. The sunlight sparked off the edge of the polished copper. The Shining Cog.

AFTERWORD

As I said in the Foreword, Scott asked me to flesh out the beliefs of the Followers of the Clockworker. I did that, and found out that it ended up being more of a religion than we'd originally planned. I also found that I'd fleshed out two other religions as well: The Followers of the Shepherd and the Carpenter.

One day I plan on going back to this world and writing more about Alex Coppersmith and his experiences along the trail as a Martial and a Judge. If you've enjoyed this story, please let me know. I'll see if I can bump it up on my list.

I hope you've enjoyed these stories. If you have, please tell me. And tell your friends.

ABOUT THE AUTHOR

Doc Coleman never dreamed of being a writer. He dreamed of being an actor, of making movies. He dreamed of going to space. He didn't dream hard enough, and ended up working in IT.

But he had a way with words, and he still wanted to tell stories.

Figuring that you don't get better at things you don't do, so he set about getting better at writing.

Doc's stories have appeared in The Ministry of Peculiar Occurrences' Tales from the Archives, the Way of the Gun Bushido Western Anthology, and the Steampunk Special Edition of Flagship magazine. In 2017 he published his first novel, *The Perils of Prague*, the first book in his series *The Adventures of Crackle and Bang*.

He is the show runner for the Balticon Podcast, and a narrator and a voice actor.

When he isn't juggling projects, making a living, or mainlining podcasts, Doc is a gamer, an avid reader, a motorcyclist, a home brewer and beer lover, a fan of renaissance festivals, and frequently a smart-ass. He lives with his lovely wife and two cats in Germantown, MD.

The Author - Doc Coleman

Did you enjoy these stories and want to know more? Want to get the most up to date information on what Doc is working on and releasing? Be sure to check out the web site, and sign up for the mailing list.

Website: https://swimmingcatstudios.com
Facebook: https://facebook.com/DocColemanAuthor/
Twitter: https://twitter.com/Scaleslea

The Cover Artist - Starla Huchton

Starla Huchton is a freelance graphic designer with experience in many various fields, including narration and being an author herself. Currently based out of Maryland, she has lived in several locations around the United States, as well as many years overseas in Iceland and Japan. As a sailor in the US Navy, she learned print shop procedures while working as a Lithographer, and experienced the design side of the house both in the military and as a civilian marketing assistant. After earning an Associates degree in Graphic Arts from Monterey Peninsula college in 2011, she opened up shop to create book covers for independent authors and small presses.

Website: https://www.designedbystarla.com
Facebook: https://www.facebook.com/CoversDesignedByStarla/

The Editor - Erin Kazmark

Erin Kazmark is the proud mother of three amazing nerds-in-training, a staunch Disney geek, a writer and editor, a ridiculously skilled seamstress, and a talented voice actress. Her voice credits include The Melting Potcast, Supervillain Corner, The Voice of Free Planet X, Cold Reads, This Kaiju Life, and the forthcoming Vampire Needed.

Twitter: https://twitter.com/emkaz87

AN EXCERPT FROM THE PERILS OF PRAGUE

THE ADVENTURES OF CRACKLE AND BANG, BOOK 1

CHAPTER 1

AN ENCOUNTER AT THE BOHEMIAN OPERA

"Faster! Faster, man! *Macht schnell! Rychleji!*" I screamed at the driver as we careened around a corner, the carriage momentarily tipping up on two wheels as we narrowly avoided colliding with a wagon going the other way.

The horses neighed as the driver cracked his whip over their sweat-covered flanks. Pedestrians scattered from our path, leaping to the relative safety of the sidewalks and lobbing curses after us. *Little do they care that my life will be utterly ruined if I am late to the opera,* I thought. I repeated my exhortation for speed in broken German and even worse Bohemian. I wasn't even sure I used the right word, but it was clear from the driver's reaction he understood my meaning.

He understood English, of course. Practically everyone in the Empire spoke English in some capacity, with the possible exception of some of the most provincial farmers. My uncle Randolph, Duke of Bohemia by marriage, always said it was best to speak some of the native language when traveling abroad. It projected the impression we came to the country as partners, not rulers. He claimed it yielded much better results with the servants, or something of that nature. I honestly didn't pay much attention to him at the time. I only recalled his advice because of frequent repetitions. Who would have thought it would turn out to be useful? Since it had, I dearly hoped I remembered it correctly.

Uncle Randolph was the reason I was leaning out the window of his fourth-best coach, racing through the gaslit streets of Prague just past twilight, and admonishing the coachman for more speed. My lady mother sent me to visit Uncle Randolph and Aunt Katerina, allegedly as the first step of my Grand Tour to celebrate the completion of my university education and my emergence into high society as an adult. In reality, it was the next step in my parents continuing plot to dictate every step of my life.

From his behavior over the past two weeks, I deduced my uncle was charged with shaping me into my parent's idea of a proper member of the noble class. That particular experiment seemed doomed, as my best efforts failed to produce any hint of approval from Uncle Randolph. His critical frowns haunted me as I staggered my way through one society function after another. I much preferred the polite dismissal I received from commoners to the vocal disapproval I continually encountered from fellow nobles.

After weeks of my uncle's tutelage, and a series of unfortunate events, I found myself clinging to the roof of the carriage to keep from falling out the window as we galloped through the streets of Prague. A twisting in my stomach reminded me the evening was likely to be my last chance to gain favor in his eyes. If I conducted myself to his satisfaction at the opera, my uncle promised to forgive my past transgressions. If not, he would cancel my tour and send me packing home to England.

I understood some of my family's objections to my wastrel ways, but they drove me to it by controlling my every move. While I admit I made mistakes, they held me responsible for many things outside of my control. It was extremely unfair of them to hold the incident with Baron Berka's daughter against me. The woman was over a foot taller than me and strong enough to carry her own horse! Frankly, it is impossible to dance while one's hand and shoulder are being crushed in a vise-like grip. And the Comte du Langres positively reeked of cheese and onions. I wasn't being rude; I was trying to catch my breath.

When Uncle Randolph sent word earlier in the day to say he would not be able to take me to The Bohemian Opera that evening, I was momentarily overjoyed. My jubilation came quickly crashing down when I read his message further and discovered he wanted me to meet him at the State Opera House, on time and properly attired.

Dressing for the evening was a disaster.

I fortified myself with a glass or two of wine to prepare for the ordeal of another evening of "culture". In retrospect, that may have been a mistake. While the wine helped calm my nerves, it did no favors for my hands and I accidentally spilled some of the beverage on my shirt, forcing me to seek out a fresh one. I then dropped one of my studs while donning the replacement. Naturally, the errant piece of jewelry skittered away from me and hid under the bed, further souring my mood. When I retrieved the damned thing, the second shirt was ruined from a streak of dirt up the length of the sleeve.

I whipped the soiled garment off to put on a third dress shirt and then couldn't find my cuff links. I lost precious minutes searching for them before I found them hiding in the cuffs of the wine-stained shirt. When I finally managed to don a shirt without ruining it, I spent a good half-hour trying to find my dress shoes, and in the end settled for my next best pair.

By the time I managed to dress myself in something close to my uncle's standards, I was horribly late and desperate to make up the time. I charged my uncle's coachman to make all haste and promised him a great deal more money than I was able to pay should he deliver me on time.

I flung myself from the coach as we pulled up in front of the opera house, not waiting for the carriage to stop, but leaping to the street at a run, clutching my top hat in one hand and staggering to keep from falling and ruining my clothes, yet again. I raced up the grand stair, which fronted the State Opera House, abandoning any semblance of dignity. The august facade of the venerable building was unmoved, although I dare say some of the passersby were alarmed by the display. Fixated upon the consequences of arriving too late for the performance, I ran for all I was worth.

I caught the door as an usher in neat grey livery pulled it closed. He blocked the way with his body and said, "I'm sorry, sir, no one is permitted to enter once the doors are closed."

"But it is not closed," I replied. "Indeed, if you will stand aside I shall be glad to assist you in sealing this portal against those who would attempt to re-open it."

The man remained unmoved. "Sir, the performance is about to begin, and for the convenience of our patrons I must ask that you remain outside." He jerked on the handle in an attempt to wrest it from my hand and trap me outside of the theatre, but I maintained my grip.

I was not about to surrender so easily. "I am one of your patrons. Indeed I have a ticket!" I reached into my jacket to produce my ticket and the man nearly slammed the door shut. I slid my foot forward to block the door and he crushed my leg quite painfully against the jamb.

"Sir, please! I must close this door!"

His unapologetic violence raised my ire. So much so I did something I previously found distasteful. Pulling myself up to my full six foot height, I looked down at him and fixed him with my most harsh and steely glare, doing my best imitation the elitist prigs who made much of my life miserable. Summoning every ounce of self-importance I could muster, I leaned forward and asked, "Do you know who I am?"

"No, sir, I do not, and it would make no difference in any case. I must close the door!"

I told him.

The man's face blanched, the blood drained from his face as his eyes widened in shock and confusion. His hands fell limply to his side. He stepped backwards, his face transformed into a twisted rictus as he shied away. I pulled the door open and slid inside, pushing past the stunned usher. Tearing my own ticket, I dropped one half of the stub into the box with a flourish. Pointing to the open door, I told the man, "You should close that before some riffraff come in."

I turned and strode rapidly away from the sputtering man before he could gather his wits and pursue me.

It was the first time in my life I was grateful for my great-grandfather's perverse sense of social humor and the shockingly obscene name he saw fit to inflict upon me. It was not to be the last.

Desperate to regain time lost with the usher, I ran up the two flights of stairs to the level of the luxury boxes. I paused for a moment to regain my composure in the cool air of the foyer to my uncle's private box. If I entered before the performance began, I could count myself as punctual, but it would not do me any good to arrive disheveled, sweating, and panting with exertion. I inhaled deeply to steady my ragged breath and coax my heart to a more leisurely pace. As I did so, I drew my hands down over my suit to restore the lines of my attire to their proper state. Finally, I relaxed the crushing grip on my top hat and straightened the brim.

Thus composed, I opened the door to the box and slipped inside as quietly as I could. It took a moment for my eyes to adjust to the dimness, but my ears instantly informed me I had made it. I successfully arrived by an acceptable margin, as the orchestra was still busy with their pre-performance tunings. I closed the door behind me and turned to find myself confronted by a couple who were complete strangers to me.

I began to stammer an apology, thinking I entered the wrong box inadvertently, when the gentleman stood and turned, adjusting his spectacles with his left hand and extending his right as he declared, "Ah! You must be Reggie's nephew! I regret old Reggie has been called away on business this evening, but he was most kind as to allow Miss Bang and myself the use of his box. He did ask me to convey his regrets to you, my boy. Oh, do forgive my manners. I am Professor Harmonious Crackle, at your service, sir. And this lovely lady is my colleague and traveling companion, Miss Titania Bang."

Ingrained habit sent my hand out to meet his, while my mind and mouth were reeling and trying to cope with the man's statements. He was not precisely disreputable, but his odd appearance made him quite unlike anyone I could imagine as an associate of my uncle.

He was older than me, but no more than thirty, yet he had the manner of someone very confident in his position and abilities. He was two or three inches shorter than I, with close-cropped blonde hair and blue eyes shining behind his glasses. His clothes were neat, but he was obviously not dressed for an evening at the opera. He wore a tweed frock coat under a white laboratory coat, both left open to allow him access to the many pockets of his black and silver checked waistcoat. I wondered momentarily how he managed to slip past the usher in such outlandish attire. His accent marked him as a fellow Englishman, but it was the only thing about him to indicate an association with Uncle Randolph.

He shook my hand with a warm, firm grip. I attempted to gather my wits to question him about his relationship to my uncle when a motion to my right drew my attention. It proved to be the lady previously introduced, Miss Bang, stepping forward to present her hand to me. Even in the dim light of the box, the sight of her took my breath and dashed what wits I managed to recover.

To say the lady was beautiful was an understatement. She was clearly in the fullest bloom of youth, and by far the most attractive woman I had met upon my travels. Her raven hair was carefully piled upon her head, but still managed to frame her heart-shaped face. Her eyes were a warm, dark brown and her lips were lush. She was attired for the opera in a stylish gown of blue silk, which clung to her shapely form and artfully accentuated her full bosom. She appeared to be a few years younger than myself, perhaps twenty-four, and moved with the smooth, flowing grace of a dancer. She seemed as fit and appropriate to her surroundings as her companion was out of place. She smiled at me in the dim light and my heart leapt as her face lit up.

She extended her hand and I dumbly took it and kissed the top of her glove. "Such a pleasure to meet you, my lord. Your uncle has been so very kind to show us such hospitality." Her voice was likewise warm and sweet, and the sound of it made my knees threaten to desert me.

I struggled to form a reply, my mouth working on its own, but failing to produce any coherent sound. I was saved when the peculiar gentleman interrupted. "Ah, they are about to begin! Here, my good fellow, take the seat of honor along with Miss Bang. We shall have plenty of time to talk after the performance."

He took my arm and steered me to the front of the box with quiet authority. As I stepped forward, I became aware of the assembled gentles arrayed in the seats below, quietly awaiting the beginning of the opera. I felt extremely conspicuous as I stood there looking out over the audience, sitting in anticipation of the first notes of the evening's entertainment. I sat hastily, my hat still clutched awkwardly in my hand. Miss Bang gracefully folded herself into the seat beside me, the scent of her perfume wafting over me and further clouding my senses. Professor Crackle deposited himself in the seat behind me.

I struggled to make sense of the situation as the gaslights dimmed. What business had pulled my uncle away? Who were these strangers who appeared so unusual, but claimed the duke's acquaintance? I stole a last glance at Miss Bang before the failing light dropped us into full darkness. *Who was this gorgeous woman?* I wondered, *And how could I manage to get closer to her?* The thought tantalized me for a moment longer, before the first strains of music sealed each of us into our own thoughts and the performance began.

www.ingramcontent.com/pod-product-compliance
Lightning Source LLC
Chambersburg PA
CBHW071917220626
47052CB00002B/390